KU-656-567

WHEN THE TRAP GOES WRONG . . .

Dempsey held his breath as he saw the door open and then through the sights he saw Makepeace. She looked frightened as she cautiously eased out of the doorway and closed the door behind her. As she turned towards the street and took the first step down, Dempsey fired.

She crashed back onto the door and fell heavily down the steps, rolling twice before she hit the pavement. She lay perfectly still, face down.

Dempsey ran along the pavement and bent over Makepeace. Then Davros pulled up in the car and Dempsey dived into the back.

He looked out at the passing shops, and he wanted to be sick as he felt the blood going sticky on his fingers, and somewhere in the distance he heard the urgent braying of an ambulance . . . and he started to shake . . .

Also available from Futura

JESSE CARR-MARTINDALE

DEMPSEY AND MAKEPEACE

Make Peace, Not War

Based on the original screenplays by
Jesse Carr-Martindale

Futura

A Futura Book

Series created by Golden Eagle Films
Novelization copyright © Jesse Carr-Martindale 1985

First published in Great Britain in 1985 by
Futura Publications,
a Division of Macdonald & Co (Publishers) Ltd
London & Sydney

All rights reserved.
No part of this publication may be reproduced,
stored in a retrieval system, or transmitted, in any
form or by any means without the prior
permission in writing of the publisher, nor be
otherwise circulated in any form of binding or
cover other than that in which it is published and
without a similar condition including this
condition being imposed on the subsequent
purchaser.

ISBN 0 7088 2717 9

Typeset, printed and bound in Great Britain by
Hazell Watson and Viney Limited,
Member of the BPCC Group,
Aylesbury, Bucks

Futura Publications
A Division of
Macdonald & Co (Publishers) Ltd
Maxwell House
74 Worship Street
London EC2A 2En
A BPCC plc Company

'It is true, I suppose, that the Americans considered that we have led them up the garden path in the Mediterranean – but what a beautiful path the soft underbelly of Europe has proved to be. They have picked peaches here, nectarines there. How grateful they should be.'

Winston Churchill
July 1943
at a meeting of the British Chiefs of Staff.

'A Latin Prelude'

Private J. Dempsey was in his twenty-second year in the summer of 1943. He was a tall man, lean and bronzed and fit. Raised on the streets and docks of New York's Lower East Side, on the balls of his feet, and street-wise. Dempsey was a tough soldier – or so he thought before he landed on the southern coast of Sicily; but on the wrong end of a Mauser .42 he quickly discovered that soiling his army issue underpants was a talent he had in common with most men half his size.

However, the advance of the American 5th Army from the southern coast to Palermo was accomplished with amazing speed, and only seven days after their landing James Dempsey the second found himself standing in the gardens of the Piazza Castelnuova. Surrounded by neo-Baroque houses and with the heady scent of success and hibiscus in his nostrils, he thought he knew what war was all about. He stood there in that early evening and the air seemed to be full of golden dust, as he looked about him in naïve wonderment at the bowl of purple and violet hills that surrounded the city, with its towers and domes and red roofs, and beyond it to the north, the deep blue of the sea. Palermo had the loveliest setting and the greatest charm for those willing to seek it out – and along with his comrades, Dempsey was about to seek out his own little piece of Sicilian hospitality. New York seemed a world away.

Dempsey's unit was to stay in Palermo for only three days before the advance to Messina. A convenient delay, some say, to allow almost the entire German and Italian forces to be plucked from the island and evacuated at the rate of 8,000 a day across the Straits of

Messina to the relative safety of the Italian mainland. But those three days would be the last time that Dempsey would be able to wallow in the peaches and nectarines of the Italian soft underbelly. The advance towards Rome with the landings at Salerno, the battle at Cassino and Anzio would be much less of a picnic than Palermo. So he wallowed for three days in the wine and women of that city, both of which were free, both of which were taken in excess. Dempsey got drunk and Maria Gambino got pregnant – in that order.

In the spring of 1944 with the horrors of the battle of Cassino still fresh in their memory, the men of the Fifth Army were preparing for the battle for Anzio. The winter in Italy had been appalling and the fighting had been bloodier than ever expected, with a casualty rate of forty-one per cent of American soldiers killed or wounded. Dempsey longed for the hard, familiar skyline of Manhattan that seemed so far away from the fox-hole in the soft Italian mud.

The attack on Anzio began on the morning of the 23rd May at 06.30 and as the artillery barrage lifted from the German defensive positions, the midwife in Palermo attending Maria Gambino rested her finger-tips on the dead mother's eyelids and closed them; for her the fight was over. A son had been born, a bastard out of wedlock and the Gambino family made a pledge that night to take their revenge on the father of the bastard if the Germans had not already saved them the trouble; and if the war didn't kill him then the Gambinos would – or the Inzerillos or the Albertis, for the Mafia has always had a weak-spot for New York – on the Lower East Side.

'Naples and Cassino, taken in our stride.
We didn't go to fight, we just went for the ride.
Anzio and Sangro are just names.
We only went to look for dames.
We're still all D-Day dodging in sunny Italy'.

*
8

On the 4th June the American Fifth Army entered Rome and two days later the Allies landed in Normandy. For James Dempsey the fighting was over and in the twelve months he learned a little Italian, gained a pretty thorough working knowledge of the raunchy neighbourhood beneath the Palazzo Farnese and put on a little weight, gaining a taste for pasta in the process.

When he returned to New York some months after V.E. day, he was Brooklyn's local hero on 67th Street and he got a great charge from sporting not only a chest full of medals, but also Sophia Dempsey – his new Italian wife, liberated by his own fair hand from the gutters of Rome.

However, Sophia was smart, smarter than Dempsey, and in Rome she had never been without the luxuries of life – German luxuries to begin with but latterly everything that the PX could come up with. Sophia knew which side her salami was buttered and lost no time in getting herself and Dempsey out of Brooklyn and over the bridge to Manhattan.

'Manhattan is better for me, Jimmy,' she would say. 'In Manhattan a girl can be someone, it's smart, you know?'

'Sure, Sophia, anything you say,' and he stroked her rump and lifted her dress and took her standing, just like he'd done the first time on the Spanish Steps, just off the Via Veneto. Then it had been for bully beef, this time was for Manhattan, and for Dempsey she'd do it anywhere – as long as the price was right.

They had a small apartment on 67th and Columbus Avenue. Nothing fancy, but it was clean and had an elevator. Dempsey drove a cab and Sophia was in daytime domestic service for a fat cat called Morganburg, who was in advertising and lived at 75 Central Park West; and that was real fancy. He had a big buck black boy who drove his Cadillac and another who pressed his pants and Sophia dusted and cooked a little and fooled around a lot – when Dempsey was working nights.

Mr Morganburg was in love with Sophia and made sure, in every possible way, she was never short of salami – but it was a one-way romance. For Sophia it was strictly business and a convenient way to supplement the wages of a New York cab driver – until, that is, she got herself pregnant.

The crisis then for Sophia was simply one of identity – was it Morganburg or was it Dempsey, and who was best for her? She wrestled with the problem for some weeks and amidst an unprecedented spate of Hail Marys and genuflecting, came to the more practical decision to tell fat cat Morganburg that he was the lucky guy. The onerous task of breaking the news to both men however never presented itself, as on the night she'd chosen to pull the rug from under Dempsey it was done for her in the Grand Manner.

Dempsey was taking his fare from Queens, over the Pulaski Bridge to Greenpoint Avenue. It was a cold night and the wipers were building the snow up on the windscreen so fast that Dempsey had to keep stopping to clean off the snow.

'Take a right,' the man in the back said, as Dempsey got back in the cab for the fourth time.

'You ain't going to Lafayette Avenue no more?' Dempsey asked, and swung the cab into the next right turn, down towards the shoreline.

'No, just head down to the river.'

Dempsey drove slowly and when he reached the East River he stopped and turned to look at the man in the back of his cab.

'Now what?' Dempsey grinned at the man. 'There's not a whole lot going on down here, where was it you wanted to go exactly?'

The man flicked open the catches on the suitcase that was on the seat beside him and grinned at Dempsey. 'So, where were you in the war, soldier boy?'

Dempsey smiled as he heard the thick Italian accent. 'Why I damned nearly liberated your country single-handed – after you'd changed sides, of course. Landed in Sicily and walked all the way up to Roma – brought me a wife home too!' He took a photograph of Sophia from his wallet but the man ignored the picture. 'Where you from, fella – down south some place?'

The man nodded. 'From Palermo.'

'Palermo – no kidding; boy I had me a ball in Palermo.'

Camelo Inzerillo opened the suitcase, took out the sawn-off twelve-bore pump and shot Dempsey's head clean off.

The wipers flailed madly in the open windscreen and the snow fell into the front of the car and onto the broken glass and the blood and what was left of Dempsey. Camelo Inzerillo slipped stones into the pocket of the dead man, replaced the shotgun into the case and hurriedly transferred himself to the black Pontiac that had followed the cab all the way from Manhattan. The Pontiac turned in the road and the red tail-lights and the tyre tracks quickly disappeared into the snow and the night. The motor in Dempsey's cab idled for two hours before it stopped, and when his body was discovered the next morning, the meter was still running.

Sophia Dempsey identified her husband by the scar on his right forearm that had been picked up in a knife fight in a bar in Sicily – 'something to do with a woman' he'd said but he'd never been specific – maybe that'd been his problem.

CHAPTER ONE

'Manhattan 1984'

Sophia Dempsey sat in the apartment on Central Park West, looking down on her 'meadow', which is what she called Central Park. Immediately below was the Tavern On the Green, shrouded in the naked trees of December, and sprinkled with what looked like a million fairy lights – it was Christmas in New York.

She listened to the muffled, familiar sounds of the city that had, for the past forty years, been her friend and her judge and now she was alone in what was an uncomfortable inheritance. The fat cat was dead and cremated and scattered, and Sophia Dempsey sat alone in her splendid legacy on the fourteenth floor and felt just a little pang of guilt. But, like all pangs, it would pass; and she smiled to herself into the picture window and at her reflection in the black sky over Queens where they'd found her husband those forty years back with the stones in his pocket, the secret signature of a Mafia killing; but she never knew why and she never would.

Sophia was in her early sixties, but despite the ravages of time and pasta, and her innumerable indiscretions with the fat cat, until he simply couldn't get it up any more, she was still in pretty good shape. She ran her hand across the glass, inspecting it for cleanliness and she nodded in silent approval both at her picture of Manhattan and then, as she turned, at her newly acquired apartment.

'Forty years on and I gotta ritzy place,' she said out loud. 'Forty years and a lotta humping,' and she placed her hands on her hips and stood leaning slightly backwards, like a fish-wife from Naples.

She looked about the apartment and gave a deep sigh, wondering if she'd be lonely. For forty years she'd come here as domestic and paramour and she knew every inch of the place – but now she wondered if indeed it would be her home. She looked at the books that lined one wall, books that not even old Morganburg had ever opened, let alone read. Thousands of dollars' worth of books and records, most of them never played, and pictures. She hated the pictures and the glass tables and the mirrored ceiling in the dining room. With a passion she hated the mirrored ceiling in the dining room. Between the dining room and a kitchen that looked more like a research laboratory, was an octagonal, walk-in wine store that was regulated to a constant temperature of 43° F.

'*Mama mia!*' she said. 'What the hell do I want with a walk-in refrigerated wine store? I think maybe I give the whole shooting match to Jimmy – it's more his style and maybe I go back to Roma and start over.' She walked through the dark blue dining room – and glanced up at herself.

'Decadent.' And she shook her head and shivered a little as she passed the wine cooler on her way to the kitchen. She would make a pot of coffee, or maybe cappucino with the special machine, and then she would sit and wait. Watch TV maybe until her Jimmy came home. It could be a long night, her son Jimmy was on a big bust, but she'd wait up. She always did. New York was a violent city and her son was in a violent profession. James Dempsey the third was a cop.

The noise of the cappuccino machine was so loud in her empty kitchen that she switched it off and made a cup of instant from the faucet that delivered boiling water, day or night. Instant! America!

'Jimmy will be okay!' she said. 'Jimmy's got the best partner in the city.' She switched on the TV. 'The best back-up boy ever,' and she sat and channel-hopped until she was certain that there was nothing worth watching. Outside, in the distance, she could hear the incessant honking of the chequer cabs and the wail of an ambulance. She got up and went to her window and looked again out across the park and beyond to Queens. She rubbed the window again as the first snow before Christmas landed unannounced on the cold outside glass, and she remembered his chestful of medals and the time she was a GI bride. The snowflakes melted on the glass and ran down the window and she tasted salt as her tears ran into the corner of her mouth, and another ambulance wailed away below her on its way down to Broadway to mop up the spilled blood of night trash.

'What a shame my Jimmy don't speak Italian – we would both go back to Roma maybe one day.'

Officer Joe Spitzer sat in the unmarked patrol car outside the headquarters of Precinct 20 on West 82nd Street. He seemed nervous and he lit another cigarette from the butt of his last and waited for his partner. Five minutes later Dempsey left the doorway of the Precinct building, crossed the street and got into the car. He chewed gum in time with his lungs and he grinned at his friend through the smoke.

'Just because you come from LA, Spitzer, don't mean you always gotta see the air you breathe. Put that goddamn thing out and let's lay some rubber!'

Joe Spitzer flipped the cigarette onto the sidewalk and drove the car into Broadway, heading south.

'Where to?'

'Go left on 43rd and then park some place.'

'We ain't going on a stake-out again – my wrap sheet's full of nothing but two-bit busts.'

Joe struck the wheel with the heel of his hand and contemplated another cold night watching black hookers freeze their fannies off and screeching abuse at the white 'tourists' who were drawn by the lure of a black fuck. 'Pink inside, just like white lady!' But the tourists were still apprehensive about herpes as a lifelong

15

companion. In New York it's a way of life – in Staines it's difficult to fool your wife about having sat on a suspect toilet seat.

Dempsey looked across at his partner of six years' standing and grinned. 'This ain't no two-bit bust, Joey – this is a big one – this one's gonna get us promoted.'

'How come it's news to me?'

'The Captain's had some asshole from the drug squad in the shadows of a guy called Schwartz.'

'Schwartz?'

'Yeah – you heard of him?'

'No.'

'Me neither – he's big time, from the West Coast.'

'I never heard of him.' Joe swung into 43rd Street and cruised until he could park.

'He's a producer – he puts deals together and takes a percentage of the take. He finds the money men, the distribution network – the end customers. In San Francisco he's the front man for the gays.'

'No kidding. That's a lotta coke.'

Dempsey nodded. 'They got more gays in San Fran than we got bagels in New York.'

'That's a lotta bagels, let's go!' and Dempsey got out of the car and felt the cold wetness of the snow on his face. He looked at his watch and wished he was back in the car. He wished he was someplace else.

The two men walked the block. Three times they passed their car and three times they were spotted – by the Armenian selling bagels on the corner of Broadway and 43rd. Dempsey stopped by the stall.

'Two,' he said abruptly, took the bagels, gave one to Joe and gave the man a dollar bill.

'Is he there?'

'Went in about an hour ago.'

'Did he come out?'

'Nope.'

'Thanks,' and Dempsey and Spitzer walked away, leaving the bagels on the stall.

'I hate bagels,' said Joe.

'Me, too,' and Dempsey grinned at his friend. 'I don't care too much for queens neither,' and he checked the traffic, crossed the street and went up the stairs into the strip joint. Joe followed him a pace behind, watching.

The girl at the desk was black with beads in her plaited hair and a big, wide mouth, that would open with the least provocation, like a switch-blade. She wore satin hot-pants, like all the hookers on Eighth Avenue, and had the tell-tale glaze on her big eyeballs. She's the kind of dame who powders her nose from the inside, Dempsey thought, as he paid up his thirty bucks and went into the darkness beyond the scruffy swing doors. Inside, about a dozen men sat around a long cat-walk and at the end of the cat-walk was a tired screen that was showing old hard porn movies between the live bouts. Dempsey and Joe sat at a table and watched the reciprocating motions of a semi-limp cock belonging to a long-haired Swede, who looked like he'd stepped out of the last decade but one. A black girl, who might have been pretty about the same time the Swede on the screen had been fashionable, sat next to Dempsey.

'Hi,' she said. 'You wanna drink?'

'Sure,' Dempsey said. 'But that's all.'

The girl looked hurt, like it should make Dempsey feel a heel but then smiled again. 'You ever had a black girl?' and she put a hand on his thigh. 'Nigger girls fuck good.'

Dempsey looked at her hand and narrowed his eyes. 'I came in outta the snow – get me and my friend a beer and then get your ass back here – you may have to eat them words.'

The girl grinned and touched him between the legs and disappeared.

Joe Spitzer looked uneasy and watched her until she was out of sight. 'Are you outta your fuckin' mind or somethin'? You go screwing black dogs like her, you're gonna wind up with fuckin' rabies!'

17

Dempsey leant across to his friend and whispered: 'Without taking me literally, I'd appreciate it if you watched my ass. There's a big hand-over going on backstage and I intend to get into the action – now all you gotta do is stop anybody from leaving, apart from these guys out here—' he nodded to the audience. 'The sooner they get out the better. Oh-oh, looks like you just got lucky.'

He saw the black girl coming back with a tray of drinks: two beers, two champagne cocktails at fifty bucks a throw – and a friend. The friend was hot-pants on the door with the switch-blade mouth. The old tired Swede jerked off into the face of his co-star, the screen crackled into blackness and a young blonde appeared on the cat-walk to the music of Marvin Gaye, who'd heard something on the grapevine.

'Vintage stuff, eh?' Dempsey said in a loud voice.

'What d'ya mean by that!' Switch-blade's mouth opened and closed like a subway door.

'I mean the music, honey – don't get so touchy,' and Dempsey smiled at the two hookers who'd seen the best side of forty some time ago.

'Cheers,' he said and toasted them both with the bottle of beer. 'Here's looking up you,' and he drank from the neck of the bottle.

Hot pants, not one to lose time, which quite clearly was not on her side, was laying out the financial deal into Joe's right ear while the other one just sat back and sipped her drink. The young blonde had dispensed with what little clothing she had in the first fourteen bars of Marvin and had started her routine with the Coca Cola bottle. Joe leaned forward across the table, his eyes popping.

'I never seen that before – with a bottle of Coke.' He shook his head as the bottle slid out of sight for the second time. 'Never blunt end first, anyhows.'

Dempsey laughed. 'You oughta see her with a six-pack, man – she makes Houdini look amateur,' and he put his hand high up on the hooker's thigh – way above the snow line. 'You got any tricks like that?'

'Buster – if you got the dough I'll stand on my head and whistle the Yellow Rose of Texas through my fanny – let's go,' and she took him by the hand and led him away from the table.

The room was more a cubicle than a room; one of several set to one side of the cat-walk. There was a handbasin with only one faucet, and not a lot had come out of that for some time. A chair and a low single bed with a horsehair palliasse that looked like it was on the move added the final touches of luxury. Hot-pants locked the door and hung her coat on the back of another door that led off to the rear of the building. She unzipped her dress, stepped out of it and turned to face Dempsey wearing only her white street boots.

'Okay, mister – tell me what it is you're here for and I'll tell you how much. Whatever it is and I'll do it,' and she lifted a white booted foot onto the chair, pulled her knee back through an arc of 90° and rubbed herself.

Schwartz was in his late thirties, well built with dark hair slicked back with brilliantine. He wore a camel coat and a grey fedora and there were still the marks of the melted snow on his shoulders. He stood in the middle of the office and on the desk in front of him was a briefcase. The top of the case was open and inside the case were a dozen or so black plastic bags, taped up and lying flat. Schwartz looked at the other two men in the room. Max Carella was behind the desk and behind him was his minder. A bull of a man with brains to match.

'Mind if I test it?'

'Go ahead,' said Carella. 'It's all grade four stuff.'

Schwartz took a black pack at random, punctured it with a nail file and dropped a minute amount of the white powder into a small bottle of clear liquid. He shook the bottle and held it up to the light. The liquid

19

had taken on a deep purple colour. He smiled and put the bottle back in his pocket, resealed the pack with a roll of adhesive tape and tapped the lid of the case.

'Looks like we gotta deal.' As he took a heavy looking manilla envelope from his inside coat pocket the door behind him opened and the hooker, still wearing her white boots, stood in the doorway. She looked scared. Schwartz spun on his heel and Max Carella stood up.

'Marleen, what the fuck are you doin'? You flipped out or something?'

She was pushed hard from behind and she stumbled into the room, falling onto Schwartz who pushed her away. Dempsey stood in the doorway, crouched low and holding his .44 Magnum in both hands, arms outstretched.

'Anybody make a move and I'll take their head off. You—' he nodded towards the hooker – 'get up and over there.'

The girl crawled on all fours to the side of the office, sobbing and shaking with fear.

'Now – everybody does as I say and we'll all walk outta here breathing – make a wrong move and you're gonna be eating hospital food for a long time on Rikers Island. Okay, now you—' he looked at Carella – 'you the boss?' The man nodded. 'Okay – sit down and pick up the phone, now – turn the phone so I can see it – and dial 799–6211.' He watched the man dial the number and heard the ringing tone.

'Ask for Captain Harvey Waissman and when he answers . . .' Dempsey stopped talking as he felt the cold steel of a .38 in his neck and his worst fear was confirmed when he heard the voice close to his left ear.

'Put the phone down, Max.'

Dempsey let his breath go in a long low sigh as he let the Magnum fall to his side and released the fingerful of trigger that he had squeezed to the second pressure. Max replaced the receiver on its cradle and Dempsey could hear the faint, anxious voice of the Captain of the 20th Precinct before communication was broken off. Max smiled, and so did his ape and Schwartz closed the lid of the briefcase.

'Good evening, I guess you must be Dempsey.' Schwartz touched the grey fedora and imperceptibly nodded beyond and behind Dempsey's right shoulder.

Dempsey stepped forward a pace into the room and heard the breathing behind him catch and then stop. As Max pulled open the drawer of his desk, Dempsey's left hand touched the edge of the open door and with all the strength he could summon, he smashed the door shut. Rolling forward on the floor into the knee-hole of the desk he fired his first round into Max's crutch, then turned and fired four rapid rounds into the flimsy pine door; and for an instant, crouched in the knee-hole of the desk, he felt safe. The black hooker screamed until her lungs emptied, broke into uncontrollable sobbing and then wet herself.

A strange stillness fell on the room, broken only by the sound of the girl sobbing. Dempsey crouched under the desk, now uncertain of his next move, but increasingly aware of his vulnerability in what was a crazy, if not bizarre, situation. He felt a movement behind him, he turned in the cramped space and saw the blood spilling freely from Max Carella's crutch. His body lay across the desk above Dempsey's head and he was grunting and spitting blood onto the blotter.

Schwartz made the first move, picking up the briefcase and the money and lunging at the shattered door. Dempsey tried to shout for him to stop, or freeze, or do anything other than leave, but his voice wouldn't work and the man didn't stop. Blindly he fired the last round in the chamber of the Magnum. The round went wide, hit the briefcase and tore it from his grasp. Grade four heroin scattered in the passage outside like a flour bag at a college rag and Schwartz was gone before it even had time to settle on the bloody warm corpse beyond the splintered pine doorway. Dempsey eased out from under the desk.

'Some fuckin' partner!' he growled, quite forgetting

about the ape. But the ape could count and he'd counted six shots, and as Dempsey tried to stand he felt a blow on the back of the neck. His vision blurred and he sank to the carpet and the ape went through the doorway as quick as a rat up a drainpipe.

Dempsey shook his head, and felt the pain that seemed to go all the way down to his feet. He knelt on all fours and looked out of the door. Outside in the passage he could hear the screaming hookers disengaging from their clients, and the footsteps of panic as whore and customer alike made their exit down the stairs to the street and the relative safety of a New York night.

He looked across the room to the sobbing woman in white boots, and then painfully he got to his feet.

'You'd better get your street clothes on, honey, 'cos pretty soon this place is gonna be crawling with the boys from the drug squad, the vice squad, homicide, you name it.' He picked up the phone next to Max Carella, who was dying on his desk in a pool of blood. Dempsey looked down at him in disgust.

'That's a helluva cough you got there, fella – I'd call a doctor – but I guess it's too late.' He punched out Captain Waissman's direct line and waited. 'Hi Captain – it's Lieutenant Dempsey – I'm fine. You want the good news or the bad news first?' He paused and looked at the body in the passage. 'Well, the bad news is that Nico Schwartz got clean away – yeah. The good news? The good news ain't so good. I just killed my partner!'

The Captain of the 20th Precinct was Harvey Waissman, and he was everything and more that typified a New York senior police officer. He was fat and he sweated a lot. He had body-odour capable of wilting an aerosol can at twenty paces and he drank – a lot. Harvey had been a cop for as long as he could remember, and always in New York. New York for him

22

held no secrets. Like he said: 'You go to bed with dogs, you wake up with fleas.'

He now crouched behind his desk like a pink toad, looking at Dempsey through inscrutable narrowed eyes.

'Another fine mess you got us in, boy wonder.' He paused to light a cigarette. Dempsey sat still, silently watching his Captain and wondering if he was smart and ugly or just plain ugly.

'Let's see what we got. We got half a million bucks' worth of grade four heroin – that's good. We got what's left of Max Carella, Forensic are still scraping his balls off the ceiling – and that's good, and we got ourself a dead cop, and that's bad, Dempsey, 'cos without the evidence of that black hooker, you may as well go for a walk into Harlem shouting nigger at the top of your voice.' He hauled himself out of his chair. 'The D.A.'s office is screaming for blood – and some of it's yours Dempsey.'

He thrust his hands into his pocket and hunched his shoulders. Outside it was morning and the light grey snow was settling in the streets. The bitterness of a New York winter was imminent. Waissman looked out of the window into the early morning. He was tired and was badly in need of a shave. He watched the scurrying dark figures down on the sidewalk of 82nd Street, hugging the buildings in an attempt to hide from the snow.

'You gotta be some meat-head to let that broad slip out the back like that.' His voice was a low growl and he turned to face Dempsey. 'I thought you was a smart cop, not some stupid rookie on his first bust!'

'Gimme twenty-four hours.'

'What the fuck you gonna do in twenty-four hours, Dempsey, apart from get one day older. You don't even know her goddamn name, for Christ's sake.' He sat down hard in his chair and looked at Dempsey.

'In twenty-four hours the D.A. is gonna be busting

23

that door down personally demanding your badge and your gun and your head, boy.'

He looked at his watch. 'Noon tomorrow. Good or bad, right or wrong, I want you back here in this office by noon tomorrow; and if you come back here without that black chick, then it's gonna be just a question of time before you're in the slammer. Okay?' He leaned forward.

'Dempsey – I believe you, a grand jury may not and sure as hell the internal boys won't. Joe Spitzer's record sheet is as clean as a cat's ass and you gotta pretty good reputation for being a little on the happy side, trigger-wise. Get going – and I wouldn't recommend that you try to sleep, you ain't got time for it. Now git . . . Oh – and be careful out there.'

Dempsey nodded, left the office and went back to his desk, aware of the uneasy atmosphere that hung over the office, and of the vacant desk space next to his own. He looked about him and one by one the heads turned away from him. He felt sick and as lonely as a rat-catcher's dog. He picked up his small book of phone numbers and left without a word. Dempsey was going to tear New York apart, but first he needed a drink.

There was a bar on East 96th Street that he knew called the Great Divide. It was a black bar, unhealthy for a white cop but Dempsey had some friends in Harlem and he guessed that if his black hooker was still breathing, she'd be hiding somewhere in the rotting verminous slum that was forever Harlem. Where the urban blight has hit with a vengeance and men with matted hair shuffle around in tatty old coats, clutching bottles of rot-gut hidden in brown paper bags with the unstoppered neck protruding, or crouch on the stoops of derelict buildings lazily drawing on joints. No-hopers.

Dempsey had a double bourbon without ice and he added to the telephone numbers in his book, but it wasn't until the end of the day that he'd even got close. Close enough to have her name and an old address up on 115th Street above an indoor market that sold questionable meat like pig ears and snouts, cow feet and hog maws, and sinister beans and bananas in every stage of decomposition, from green to rotten.

Someone knew her, someone had seen her, but not today, not last week. Dempsey began to worry more than somewhat. Time was not on his side for he knew that he wasn't alone in his search; there were others just as keen to silence the voice he wanted. Keener maybe. It was gone midnight when he got the beginnings of a break. She'd been seen getting out of a cab with a suitcase, a heavy suitcase, and had gone into a semi-derelict tenement block off Lexington. Dempsey got a cab with a black driver. White drivers don't wait for no-one in Harlem.

'Wait here,' he said to the cabby, and to be on the safe side made a note of the cab number. 'You lite outta here, fella, and I'll bust your ass. I may need to leave in a hurry, okay?' The driver nodded, but wasn't happy. Nobody's happy in Harlem.

Dempsey got out of the cab and walked across the street. Splinters of glass shone through the grey slush on the side-walk and the garbage of decades poked through the snow in the gutters. He squeezed between two abandoned windowless cars and noticed a man asleep in the backseat of one of the cars. The snow had drifted in through the off-side window, covering part of his body in a thin film of white powder.

He stopped by the car, some fifty yards from the front entrance to the tenement block, and something told him to wait. Behind him two headlights stabbed at the dark street and a chequer cab cruised past, looking for a number. It stopped outside the entrance. Dempsey opened the door of the car with the occupant, and got in. He sat for a minute behind the broken wheel and waited. The cab sounded its horn a couple of times and then the driver switched off the motor and it was strangely quiet.

Dempsey looked across the street at the parked cab

that had brought him here and then, with an almost casual interest, he inspected the man in the back of the car. He wasn't breathing and Dempsey wondered how long he'd been there – and how long he'd been dead.

The door of the tenement opened and he turned away from his dead travelling companion to see the woman, Marleen, leave the weak light of the doorway, half lifting, half dragging a suitcase. She made for the waiting cab and Dempsey got out of the car and walked quickly towards her. As she got to the cab, the rear door burst open and two men jumped her. She fell to the ground with a scream that was cut off as a big black hand clenched hard round her mouth and the other man rammed a syringe and needle through her coat into her arm.

Before Dempsey could get to her the cab had started off down the street with the two men in the back. It had taken five seconds. Dempsey yelled at his cab from over the street and when it stopped by him he bundled Marleen and her suitcase into the back.

'You want the new hospital?' The cabby's eyes were extra white. 'Looks like she's been O.D'd.'

'Hospital my ass – West 82nd, 20th Precinct and you gotta pink ticket for traffic violations. So hit the gas pedal!'

Dempsey cradled her head in his arms as the yellow cab bounced over the pock-marked streets of the West Side, and he saw the fear of death in her eyes.

'They got me,' she said. 'You gotta get me to a hospital.' She was already feverish and sweating hard. The needle man had hit a vein, even through the sleeve of her coat, and Dempsey guessed that he was probably a dropped-out medic.

'First you gotta see my Captain and tell him how it was last night – then we can think about hospital.'

'I gotta go now – tell the man!' She started to struggle, her eyes bulging with fear as she tried to reach for the cab driver. He turned in his seat and looked at Dempsey with black disgust.

26

'You gonna take her to hospital, man?'

'Nope. West 82nd.' And Dempsey took out his .44 Magnum and pulled back the hammer. 'That's an order.' He turned to Marleen.

'I get my Captain in the back of this cab and you tell him how it was last night; we'll be halfway to the Bellevue Hospital and you'll be fine – is that a deal, or do I pitch you out, back into the gutter?' She nodded weakly and began to shake.

'They take anyone at the Bellevue, and they don't ask questions. Shot up cops, UN diplomats; hell they even took John Lennon there – you'll be in good company.' And he turned back to the driver and snarled, 'You can drive faster than this—' and then more confidentially, 'if she goes into coma before we get there, you're gonna be picking pieces of me outta your teeth for weeks – y'understand?'

Captain Harvey Waissman listened to her almost incoherent account of the previous night, made a few notes in the back of the car and looked at Dempsey through his narrowed pig-eyes.

'You got lucky, but I ain't so sure about your friend.' He looked down at the wide-eyed stare on the woman's face.

'I don't reckon she'll be giving any live testimonies from the witness stand. But I got enough.' He sat back, away from the woman who was shaking again.

'When you're finished at Bellevue, you'd better get some rest. I wanna see you first thing tomorrow in my office.' He leant forward and tapped on the driver's grille. 'And if you don't get this fuckin' cab airborne I'm gonna hold you personally responsible for this woman's death. You dig, asshole.' The Captain had a way with words.

27

CHAPTER TWO

The dark-leaved yew trees that bordered the church-yard were heavy with rain, and the muffled verses of *Abide with me* that came from within seemed somehow contained. It was a very private affair, and even the small knot of reporters, huddled in the doorway of the pub opposite, seemed embarrassed by their own presence. There was, however, a small contingent of uniformed police strategically placed around the churchyard, just in case the embarrassment of the Press wore off when the coffin emerged from the church.

Inside, the mourners were family, friends and colleagues – some uniformed, some in plain clothes but all sharing in the grief of the mother and father of the young policeman. The policeman had been shot whilst rescuing his partner from their burning vehicle after colliding with a stolen security truck. His partner escaped with concussion and minor burns, the gang of three who had stolen the security truck disappeared into thin air, leaving the truck and its contents intact, but Detective Constable Raymond Muir took two twelve-bore cartridges in the chest at point blank range. He died in an ambulance on his way to hospital with his partner holding his hand. It seemed such a waste.

The doors of the old church opened, the Reverend Peter Clarke led the procession out of the church into the rain to the freshly dug grave that now seemed such an ugly scar on the wet grass, but soon the grass and weeds and worms would help camouflage the fresh grave, and it would become just like all the rest.

Six pall-bearers carried the coffin towards the yellow slabs of clay that were heaped to the side of the grave. Two of them were his elder brothers, two of them were his closest friends and two were members of S.I.10: Chief Superintendent Spikings, his boss, and Detective Sergeant Makepeace, his partner. The coffin made its way to the graveside slowly and with some difficulty, and at a somewhat alarming angle, for Detective Sergeant Harriet Makepeace was only 5 ft. 3 ins. – the minimum height for a policewoman.

Even though their progress was slow, the arrival at the graveside came quick enough, and the mourners gathered round, unaware of the rain and the biting cold, to look on the wet coffin; and then it was gone. Down into the cold clay that was to be his companion, so suddenly, so unexpectedly. The ashes and the dust, so expertly dispensed by the senior undertaker, had turned to mud on the polished top of the coffin before even the first hollow thuds of slab-yellow mud hit the hollow box.

Gordon Spikings put his arm around Harriet's shoulders.

'Time for a drink, eh Harry?' and he led her away down to the latch gate and his car. They drove in silence back to London and had a drink, and then he took her home and she cried on his shoulder before she went in.

As he drove away from her flat the day had faded and he switched on the car's lights. It was Friday the 21st. The shortest day. Next week would be Christmas. Shit. He parked in Soho Square on a yellow line and went for another drink. Somebody else could look after the 'shop' – it was the shortest day, after all.

The 'shop' was on the edge of a light industrial estate built in the Fifties, halfway between New Cross and the Elephant and Castle. There was a To Let sign in the window and nothing visible that could compromise the identity or occupation of the tenants. The boys of S.I.10 were very special, very good and not very nice to know. Spikings got back to his office in the early evening, just very slightly the worse for wear and slightly meaner than usual as a result. He snatched

29

the long telex message from his deputy as he marched through the clutter of the busy outer office.

'What's all this crap, Morris – looks more like a bloody laundry list than a message,' and he swept past into the relative quiet of his own office. He sat heavily at his desk, lit a cigarette and squinted at the telex. Some five minutes later, after he'd read the contents twice, Morris appeared in the doorway with a large mug of hot sweet tea.

'Tea, guv?'

'Ta, Morris – er – you've read this, I take it?'

'Yes, sir.'

'What d'you make of it?'

'Don't like it, sir – not really our style.'

'Hmm. I think I'll have a word with the Commander.'

'What, now, sir?' Morris was apprehensive and Spikings noticed.

'What d'you mean "now"?' Spikings narrowed his piggy little eyes at Morris and pushed back the tough, grey, short-cropped hair, which instantly rearranged itself as before.

'I mean, sir, that you've had a few and our dear Commander might, just might, rumble you.' He added as an afterthought, 'With respect, sir.'

'Hmmm.' Spikings looked at Morris and then grinned. 'I suppose you're right, you bloody Scottish wog. You nearly always are.'

Morris's mother had been brought up in Glasgow and had married a sailor whose father had come from Kingston, Jamaica. So Morris had an interesting mongrel quality. But despite his very shaky start in life – for being a quarter-black kid in the Gorbals isn't exactly the recipe for a well-adjusted childhood – he managed somehow to retain his dignity, all his teeth, and a sense of humour.

'It was like being born with a silver spoon in ma mouth,' he'd say. 'Except the bastard went in sideways!' And he'd grin a grin even a blind man could see in the dark. Spikings liked him, he was a good

30

man to have around when times were tough, and those times in S.I. 10 were almost daily.

'How'd it go?'

Spikings sniffed and sipped his tea. 'Like all funerals, I s'pose – down.'

'I thought heaven was up,' and Morris grinned so hard the room got lighter.

'You know, Morris, if you could keep that up after dark, this department's electricity bills would drop considerably . . . What's been on today then? Tell me what little gems of human malfunction I've missed during my day out in the country.'

'Nothing today, guv – it's been as quiet as . . .'

'The grave? Very funny, Morris – I must bury more of my young officers – anything for a quiet life eh?'

'Sorry, guv,' and changing the subject, 'how's 'arry?'

'Flaky, Morris – very flaky. Mind you, I'm not surprised. That's two partners she's lost in six months – she's blaming herself for both of them.'

'D'you reckon she'll be okay?'

'I think so – upper-class tarts are all as tough as ingrowing toenails. It'll take a few days – maybe longer – but she'll be okay, you'll see.' He paused and looked down at the telex message. 'Maybe she would be able to handle this little bombshell – it might be just what she needs to get 'er back on stream. What d'you think?'

Morris winced and thumbed something from his nose.

'Well, you can tell 'er, guv. Not me.'

Lord Winfield sat at the head of his dining table and smiled at his daughter, who was looking desperately depressed. He got up, wandered to the window and looked out across the road to the headquarter building of the St. John Ambulance, that once had been a private house, like all the houses in Eaton Place. Now they were all flats or offices and most of the residents were foreign.

'Old Tubby Duckworth used to live in that house –

31

when it was a house,' he said, and his voice trailed away as he realized the insignificance of the remark. He ran his hand up the edge of the casement window and felt the cold London air fairly breezing through the old loose-fitting window.

'Hell of a bloody draught through these windows.' He paused. 'Should get that double-glazing stuff, I s'pose, you can drop a feather when there's a helicopter revving up on yer lawn – bloody silly eh?'.

Harriet looked at her father and felt sorry for him and his inability to comfort her when she needed just a bit of the milk of human kindness.

'D'you ever regret that I was born a girl, Daddy?' she said and wiped away what she promised herself was the very last tear. 'I mean, Oxford Blue at rowing and cricket; Sandhurst; Long Range Desert Group in Africa then home with a bucketful of medals, and after trying like an old stoat for years and years – you wind up with me.'

She pushed her chair away from the other end of the table and watched her father. He rattled the window a bit and then turned, and she saw for the first time ever a wetness in his bright blue eyes. Checked and under control, running absolutely no risk of running out of the sunken old sockets, but nevertheless there. He smiled at her, like he used to smile at her mother, and moved across the room until he stood behind her. She felt his hands on her shoulders and the old tough fingers grip hard through the soft grey leather of her jacket.

'You must never think that, Harry old gal,' he said. 'I couldn't be happier or prouder of you than I could if I had a whole teamful of sons at Twickers at a Varsity match.' He kissed the top of her head and then let go.

'Fancy a port? I've got a nice bottle of "crusted" that I decanted at luncheon – do you good,' and then he touched her shoulder again. 'C'mon, old girl, it'll take some of the hurt away. Can't bring him back, y'know.'

32

She put her hand on his and looked up at her old war-horse of a father.

'Stiff upper lip eh. Par for the course and all that.'

'Something like that – but I warned you. Police work in a capital city is a dangerous and thankless task, and it doesn't matter which city it is or where in the world it is. Criminals can only exist where there's money and despite rumours to the contrary, London's a bloody rich place. Come, let's finish the port, and then you can decide whether you go back to your flat or stay here with the old man.'

She stood up and they linked arms.

'I think I might like that,' she said, as they walked from the dining room and he wished that his only child had chosen a slightly less dangerous profession. She was strikingly good looking, and after an almost arranged marriage to a barrister, tipped by most in Lincoln's Inn Fields for the top, Lord Winfield had felt rather confident about his daughter's security and of himself becoming a grandfather. But it was not to be, and the only thing that came out of the marriage was a rather smart flat in Hampstead and an overwhelming desire to become the first female Commissioner for the Metropolitan Police.

She sat on the carpet by the fire, sipping a rather large glass of port.

'You're obviously hellbent on keeping me here against my will, aren't you?' she said, inspecting the port. 'I certainly won't be fit to drive anywhere after this, and I know how you hate leaving the place cluttered up with half empty decanters.' She looked up at her father and pushed the blonde hair from her eyes.

'I'm all right, you know. And it would be pretty strange if I wasn't riddled with guilt. I know it wasn't my fault – but I was the one driving the car and I was the one who crashed the bloody thing. If we hadn't had that pile-up and if our car hadn't caught fire, then

33

none of this would have happened and Raymond would still be in one piece.' She shrugged her shoulders, drank the port and looked into the fire.

'You can't go through life starting sentences with "if". Here, give me your glass. I'll get Blake to turn down your old bed.' He opened the door and yelled for his manservant. 'I must get that blasted bell fixed – it's so uncouth to have to shout for one's butler, don't you think?'

Harriet grinned. 'It's pretty uncouth these days to even have a butler. Anyway, Blake's more of a chum than a servant, surely. How long is it that he's been with you – since 1943?'

'November '42 he joined the unit, and I chose him for my batman after he'd done six months with us.'

'That's forty-three years, Daddy! – you can't have someone around for forty-three years and still call them by their surname and regard them as a servant, surely.'

The old man sniffed an embarrassed sniff and yelled again. 'Blake, where the devil are you!'

Blake appeared, stooped and somewhat out of breath.

'Sir?' he said with an indifferent tone that suggested he wasn't the least bit bothered about Lord Winfield's impatience.

'Make up the bed for Miss Harriet and make sure we've got something for breakfast tomorrow, will you?'

'I took the liberty of switching on Miss Harriet's electric blanket an hour ago, sir, and there's no problem with breakfast, sir – if you'd care to tell me what Miss Harriet and yourself would like for breakfast I'll make sure it's there, sir.'

'The trouble with you, Blake, is you're too bloody smart by half – anyway what took you so long, eh?'

Blake looked slightly bored, as though he'd had the same sort of conversation many times before.

'It's the stairs, sir – I don't seem to be able to get up 'em as fast as I used to.'

'Why's that then?'

'The arthritic hip, sir, it makes it difficult.'

'Didn't you get some pills or something for that? I seem to remember you got some pills, Blake.'

'They were for the blood pressure, sir, not the hip.'

'Good God man, you're falling apart at the seams.'

Harriet stood up and called to the two old men at the doorway. 'Why don't you come in, you two, and help me finish off this decanter of port.' Her father turned quickly to face her.

'I beg your pardon, Harriet?'

'I said, why don't you ask Mr Blake to come in and have a glass of port, Daddy. It sounds to me as though you should be looking after him, not the other way round, and anyway, it's nearly Christmas.' She poured a third glass of port and held it towards Blake who was hovering by the door. 'Come on, Mr Blake, come in and cheer me up, and Daddy stop looking like that. If you ask me, you two old duffers ought to muck-in together. Mr Blake should move upstairs and you should get in a home help to look after the pair of you.'

The two men looked at one another, both taken aback by Harriet's speech. Lord Winfield nodded his head at Blake, indicating to him that he should take the offered glass of port.

'You'd best come in, Blake,' he said confidentially.

'That's most kind of you, sir,' and Blake shuffled into the centre of the room and took the glass of port from Harriet.

'Thank you, Miss Harriet. I was very sorry to hear about your partner, Miss, very sorry indeed.'

'Yes – becoming a bit of a habit I'm afraid. Two in six months isn't exactly a good track record, is it?'

'Now, now, Harriet,' chipped in her father. 'Let's hear no more. I'm sure that's not what your Superintendent thinks.'

'Spikings!' Harriet laughed. 'I reckon he's already got me down for a desk job in traffic control by now – I seem to have rather a terminal effect on his young

35

detectives. Anyway,' she raised her glass, 'cheers, Blake, here's to 1985.'

Blake raised his glass. 'To a new partnership, Miss.'

'I beg your pardon?' Lord Winfield said quickly.

'I meant for Miss Harriet, sir.'

'Oh yes, quite, thought for an awful moment you meant something else.'

CHAPTER THREE

Ed Zukko stood slightly behind Captain Waissman. He was a small man, slightly balding and very short-sighted. He wore a crumpled, lightweight suit, which for a bad New York winter seemed kinda crazy to Dempsey. Zukko was gazing out of the Captain's window and across the street to the opposite building. He had a faraway look in his narrow eyes that squinted behind the thick lenses of his spectacles, and his face had a faint yellowish hue, like jaundice.

Waissman felt uncomfortable in the silence. He didn't like the little yellow man who stood quietly behind him, and he shifted his large frame in the complaining chair. The chair groaned as the mass of flesh rearranged itself like hot fudge on a sundae, and Dempsey knew that one day his Captain would unwittingly force a submission from the chair and both he and the chair would wind up in the accounts department one floor below.

Zukko turned away from the window and looked at Dempsey in such a way that Dempsey felt the hairs on the back of his neck stand up. Zukko smiled an inscrutable smile which vanished as quickly as it came.

'You see the thing is, Dempsey, you've left us with a bit of a problem, killing Max Carella an' all.'

Dempsey shrugged. 'How come?'

'Well, Carella was a big man in the Family, and those boys don't take too kindly to one of their top men getting blown away by a cop. Like they make sure that the cop gets eaten alive.'

'I'm still here.'

'Oh sure, maybe six months from now you'll still be here; but have no fear my friend, sooner or later they'll get you.' He leant on Captain Waissman's desk and

37

looked hard at Dempsey. 'And let's face it, Dempsey, your family ain't got too good a thing going with the Mafia.'

'You know about my father?'

'Sure, what the fuck d'you think all those assholes do all day at Langley, Virginia. They got more computers and records and files down there than the whole of the goddamn I.R.S. put together. Buster, the day you register with herpes, give us forty-eight hours and it'll be on your file – that's what the C.I.A. is all about man – information.'

Dempsey shifted uneasily in his chair, in sympathy with his Captain.

'So what now?' he asked.

'Agent Zukko here has gotta plan. Sounds kinda crazy to me but . . .'

'Dempsey – the bust with Schwartz and Carella that you stumbled into was the end of a long chain of drug trafficking that starts in Laos. I've spent the last three years in the Far East watching and recording the progress of this one particular route, and we've now got as much information as we need to mount an operation that would take out all the senior management in one move. In Cambodia, Bangkok, Istanbul, Amsterdam, here and LA. But there's one link in the chain that's not complete.'

'And that's where I come in?'

'Sure.' He shrugged. 'You're gonna get blown out anyway, Dempsey – so you may as well take a few of 'em down with you.'

'You seem pretty sure of that, Zukko.'

Zukko smiled again. 'Let's put it this way – unless there's been a change in house-rules that I don't know about, I wouldn't make any plans about retiring to Miami.'

'So where's this missing link, Zukko? Where have I gotta go to get to the happy hunting grounds?'

Captain Waissman pushed a manilla file across the desk to Dempsey. 'It's all in there, Dempsey – you can

38

read it on the plane. Right now, you'd better get home and pack. You could be away for some time.'

'Oh,' Zukko smiled again. 'I've made all the necessary arrangements for you to carry your sidearms when you're there, and,' as an afterthought, 'don't bother to pack your Bermuda shorts – it ain't that hot even in the summer. If you're still around by then, that is.'

'The ticket and flight schedule are in the back of the file.' Waissman held out his hand. 'Good luck, Dempsey. If it all fouls up, don't blame me. It wasn't my idea, but like the man says, if you're gonna go out like the 4th of July, you may as well take a few with you.'

Dempsey picked up the folder and took Waissman's hand.

'So long, sir.' He nodded to Zukko, but Zukko was looking out of the window again and so he left the office, left his desk and left the building.

In 82nd Street he got a cab and as the cab drove down Broadway, Dempsey opened the file and at the back found the airline ticket. It was a British Airways' flight from J.F.K. to Heathrow, first class. The cab stopped outside Martin's Bar where Broadway runs into Columbus Avenue and Dempsey got out.

'Hi, Jimmy!' the bartender shouted to him as he came in.

Dempsey waved at the man, sat at the bar and ordered a large vodka Martini without the olive, and without even looking at the man next to him.

'You takin' vacation?' The bartender nodded at the red, white and blue ticket that stuck out from the file.

Dempsey grinned and flipped the ticket to the man behind the bar. 'Nope.'

The man opened the ticket. 'Heathrow, that's England ain't it?'

Dempsey nodded. 'Sure is.'

'I ain't never been there.'

'Me neither.'

'When you coming back?'

'I dunno – it depends on how long it takes – I guess the ticket's open.'

The barman scrutinized the ticket and shook his head. 'You ain't coming back, Jimmy – it's one way.'

Dempsey snatched the ticket from him. 'It's what?' He looked at the details and then dropped the ticket onto the bar. 'Son of a bitch!' He spat out the words in a low growl, drank the Martini in one and pushed the glass back to the barman.

'Same again?'

Dempsey shook his head. 'No – I gotta pack and say ciao to my ma – see you, Benny.'

Benny looked after him as he pushed open the glass swing doors and turned left up towards his mother's apartment on Central Park West.

'Crazy guy,' said Benny as he took the empty glass from the bar. 'Can I get you another?'

The man at the bar nodded and Benny poured another beer.

'I used to know his old man, he's just the same. Crazy.'

Benny leant across the bar and lowered his voice. 'His old man got blown away.' He put his fingers to his head like a gun. 'Some say it was Mafia, but I ain't so sure.'

The man sipped his beer, and then lit a cigarette. He was about forty, dark-haired and smartly dressed, and in his lapel he wore a yellow rose.

'Your friend – he is going to London?'

'Yeah. You know it?'

'A little.'

The barman looked at the man and tilted his head to one side, as if inspecting a portrait.

'You gotta problem?' the man said, with just a hint of aggression in his voice.

'No – hell, I'm sorry – it's just that,' he pointed to the doorway, 'you and him – very similar in looks you know?'

*

Spikings stood in the small, private crew lounge at Heathrow and watched the fragile Lear-jet touch down hesitantly, like a dragonfly on a millpond. It was a cold, wet, Tuesday morning, New Year's Day, and Spikings looked at the dusty, tarnished Christmas decorations; dusty and tarnished from last year or even the year before that, and he rubbed his eyes and face and wished the hangover would go quickly. The New Year's Eve party at S.I.10 had been a vicious affair, and he was thankful that the event was only annual.

He walked out onto the glistening tarmac and felt the wind bite at his face, pulling at the small piece of tissue paper that held the blood at bay from the razor cut on his chin. Hangovers, new years and new blades didn't mix well for Gordon Spikings. The tissue paper flapped in the wind and tried to detach itself from the congealed blood. He pressed it back with his thumb and hoped it would stick. Meeting a Yankee policeman with a dripping chin wouldn't give the best first impression.

The small door swung up and open and collapsible steps flopped out like a tongue. Dempsey stood in the narrow, curved doorway and smiled at Spikings. It was the kind of smile that Spikings took an instant dislike to. It said, 'My name's Dempsey, I'm a wise guy – you must be Spikings and you've cut your chin.' Dempsey stepped from the cocoon onto the tarmac and hunched his shoulders from the cold drizzle. The two men stood looking at one another for a moment and then Dempsey took one pace forward.

'Do we shake hands, or do I kiss the ground?'

'Don't tell me, Dempsey – your mother's Italian.'

'You got it.'

'Then you'd be better advised to kiss my arse,' and he turned on his heel and walked back to the building with his hands thrust deeply into his overcoat pockets.

Dempsey followed a few paces behind. 'Now look here, Spikings . . .'

Spikings stopped and turned to Dempsey. 'No. You listen to me – this visit of yours is highly irregular, fraught with disaster, and if you want my professional opinion – doomed to failure. I don't want you here, Dempsey, but there's someone in the Home Office that does, so that's that. But let's get one thing straight. I run things around here, and S.I.10 is a very special bunch of people. You will fall in line with the way I run things and in return we will afford you all the help, protection and assistance that is necessary. Oh – and by the way – you address me as sir. Got it?'

'You're the boss.'

'You've got it in one, sonny – this way,' and Spikings continued on his way to the building, leaning into the wind and rain and wishing like hell he'd stayed in bed.

The silver-grey Granada pulled out of Heathrow and drove quickly up the M4 into London. The two men sat silently in the back for some time.

'I thought you were coming on a scheduled flight.' Spikings broke the silence that had lasted all the way to Hammersmith.

'I was but it got switched at the last minute by some agency guy.'

'Ed Zukko?' Spiking's question was a statement.

'Yeah. You know him?'

'Ed and I worked in the Far East together. Hong Kong mainly – I know Ed all right. He's a good man.'

'You could have fooled me,' Dempsey said, but Spikings said no more until the car slid into the rear car park of S.I.10.

'Where the hell's this?' Dempsey looked about him in surprise as Spikings got out of the car.

'This is home, Dempsey – this is home.'

'Low profile stuff, huh?'

'Sewer level, friend – where the rats are,' and Spikings walked to a black door, punched a series of numbers in a keyboard mounted on the wall and opened the door. He looked over his shoulder at Dempsey and there was just a flicker of a smile on his face.

'Come and meet the animals,' he said. 'You can leave all your gear in the motor – it'll be quite safe.'

Dempsey closed the car door and followed Spikings into the building. He followed his new boss down a dirty margarine-coloured corridor past anonymous grey doors. Spikings stopped at the end of the corridor, by a line of public telephones individually shrouded in Perspex acoustic covers.

'Oh, by the way – I'm sorry if I appeared a little short earlier – we had a bit of a thrash here last night and the head's not what it used to be.'

Dempsey nodded. 'Don't apologize – I gotta feeling we're gonna get on just great.'

Spikings blinked in surprise at the newest and most reluctant member of his élite. 'You do?'

'Sure – I'm as much a bastard as you are – sir.'

Heads in the outer office of S.I.10 were all bowed and there was very nearly an audible throb from the common hangover that had brought about a visible deceleration to quarter speed. Makepeace sat very still and even when Spikings came in she continued to nurse her splitting head by maintaining its activity at minimum.

Spikings turned to Dempsey. 'As you can see the nerve centre of S.I.10 is temporarily out of commission due to a communal brain haemorrhage that was self-inflicted last night.'

His voice rose slowly as did the heads of S.I.10. 'However – that was last night and last night was 1984. Today, gentlemen and Makepeace, is 1985. Your hangovers were acquired last year. So let's get our arses into gear, our thumbs from up our bums and our brains out of neutral, shall we!' and he swept into his office and beckoned to Morris as he went.

'Morris, in here.'

43

Dempsey stood in the middle of the office and grinned at Makepeace. She smiled back weakly, and hoped she didn't look as dreadful as she felt. Dempsey looked at the empty desk next to hers and then sat on the corner of it.

'Mind if I sit down?'

'Make yourself at home,' she said and nodded to the empty chair.

'My name's Harriet Makepeace by the way, Harry for short. You must be Dempsey.'

He sat down and rested his elbows on the desk. 'What rank are you, Harry?'

'Detective Sergeant.'

'Well, Detective Sergeant – I'm a lieutenant and there's nothing short for that, okay?'

'That's fine by me, Lieutenant.' She used the English pronunciation rather pointedly. 'And rank is so much nicer to pull if at first you demonstrate its correct pronunciation, don't you think?'

Before he could reply Spikings's head appeared round the doorway of his office. 'Harry, a moment please.'

'Excuse me – Lieutenant,' she purred, and left Dempsey with an unformulated reply to her last rapier remark. He watched her rear-end twitch its way into Spikings' office then the door shut and she was gone. Dempsey looked around the room at the faces that all seemed to wear a permanent grin.

' 'arry can be a bit lah-di-da when she puts 'er mind to it. Best to take no notice really.'

Dempsey eyed the man with a degree of contempt, but before he could respond another officer spoke.

'She's a bit touchy at the moment – lost her partner the week before Christmas. 'E got gunned down in the street so she's a bit, you know, iffy.'

'I didn't know.'

'She'll be all right, she just needs a bit of help, that's all – you weren't to know.'

Dempsey turned away from the inquisitive eyes of

44

the rest of the team, looked at the empty desk and thought about Joe Spitzer and his empty desk back at 82nd Street.

Makepeace sat in front of Spikings and Morris leant on the window-sill with one eye closed, as if waiting for an explosion.

Spikings was talking: '. . . So it's not as though it's going to be a long time, 'arry. It's not what you could call a permanent arrangement, now is it?'

'But why me?' she said. 'There's a whole roomful of blokes out there, who'd leap at the chance of giving him the run-around. Give him to one of them,' and then enthusiastically, 'give him to Big Mac, he'd sort him out. I've only spoken one sentence to the man and that was enough for me. He's awful. Anyway I presume you want to send him back to the Big Apple in one piece. If he stays with me he'll go back in bits, my record's not that good.'

' 'arry, save yer breath. It's all arranged. You and the cowboy are partners and that's all there is to it. Now you either accept my decision with good grace and get on with it or you can take it up with the Commissioner – the choice is yours.'

'Do I have one?'

'No.'

'That's rather what I thought, but there's one condition.'

Spikings raised an eyebrow. 'Condition?'

'Yes – you tell him to stop all the rank crap. As far as I'm concerned, I'll be as nice as pie to him as long as he doesn't try all the "lootenant" business, because that's really going to get up the old nostrils.'

Spikings grimaced. 'Has he started that old codswallop?'

'He has, and I don't like it.'

'Nor do I – I'll see that it's not repeated. Okay?'

'Okay.' She blew out a lungful of air and gave Spikings one of those smiles that made men's knees go weak. 'Wheel him in and break the sad news – does he know that we . . .'

'No. Not yet – er – Morris, show 'im in, would you, and bring three cups of coffee, there's a good lad. We may as well make the lootenant feel at 'ome, eh?'

Dempsey sauntered into the room and sat next to Makepeace. He nodded to Spikings and looked slightly sheepish as he caught Makepeace's eye. She was looking as haughty as she knew how, and that was pretty haughty.

'I'm sorry about your partner,' he jerked a thumb in the direction of the outer office, 'I guess I was a little out of line – I'm sorry. I know how you feel. I just lost one myself.'

Makepeace softened visibly. 'Oh – I'm sorry too – how did it happen?'

'I shot him.'

She looked stunned. 'Do you shoot many of your partners?'

'Nope – only when they try and shoot me first – I'll tell you about it later. Now, if you wouldn't mind, Sergeant, the Chief and I have gotta talk, so maybe you . . .'

Spikings interrupted. 'Sergeant Makepeace can stay, Dempsey.'

'What's she gonna do, take notes or what?'

'No – she's not going to take notes – she's going to be your partner.'

Dempsey's eyes narrowed and he put his head to the side.

'Chief, are you losing your marbles – she's a dame – I ain't gonna pair up with no dame.'

'You'll do as you're told, Dempsey, or your embassy will be informed of your non-cooperation and you'll start the first day in England with the biggest roasting you've ever had.' He pulled his chair closer to the desk.

'Now listen to me, Dempsey – I'm only going to say this once. While you're here you will conduct yourself as I request, with whom I request – at all times. And

46

for the record you and Sergeant Makepeace as far as I'm concerned, are equals. So as a guest of Her Majesty, you can forget all about being a lootenant and concentrate on being part of my organization. Now if that's not crystal clear then let me know and I'll spell it out for you. Sergeant Makepeace – 'arry to us – is one of our best operators, despite her looks, and she's also got a considerable amount of grey-matter keeping her pretty little ears apart – so remember – there's nothing dumb about this broad.'

He sat back and allowed the sermon to sink in. Makepeace shifted uncomfortably in her chair and Dempsey fixed Spikings with a piercing gaze.

'I hear what you say – but I'm telling you right now that there's not a lotta room for error. My assignment is tight and we ain't dealing with amateurs.' He turned to Makepeace. 'Have you any idea why I'm here?'

She shook her head. 'No, but I presume you're now about to tell me.'

Dempsey sighed. 'Okay, here goes,' and he paused. 'Is there any chance of any coffee, Chief – this could take some time.'

Spikings nodded as Morris came back into the office carrying a tray and four cups of coffee.

'By the way, Dempsey, if you could resist the temptation to call me Chief, I'd be much happier – it makes me feel like a petty officer. Just stick to sir, and you won't go far wrong – now pray continue. I'm sure 'arry here is all ears.'

47

CHAPTER FOUR

A battered old Ford Transit drove slowly up Wembley Hill Road and turned right, past the Stadium and into an untidy, rambling industrial estate. It was past midnight and the three occupants of the vehicle leant forward, almost pressing their black faces up against the windscreen, as they looked for the warehouse of *Action Video*.

Ziggy, Winston and Thomas were all from Jamaica, and as they huddled in the front of the cold cab their thoughts were more on Montego Bay or Spanish Town than Wembley or Kilburn. The cold bit into their thin denim jackets as they peered into the darkness and they could feel the English January through the soles of their cheap trainers, as the transit made its way past sheet metal workshops and motor accessory warehouses. Under their Fair Isle knitted woollen hats, that looked like small pullovers for evacuee children in the Blitz, the dreadlocks of the Rastafarian were crammed reluctantly, offering little protection for the snakes of the three gorgons.

Winston sat in the middle, holding a small transistor radio to his ear and swaying in time to Bob Marley. Ziggy drove and Thomas watched, beating in subsidiary time with the reggae.

'When I got enough readies it's gonna be goin' home time for me.' Winston swayed with the radio as if it were welded to his head. 'And it's gonna be Alligator Pond Bay, with de warm Caribbean sea knocking on de door, yes, man; an' all them rich whites from New York and Boston wanting a bit of black dick.' He grinned and pointed between his legs, 'And I got de answer hanging down here.'

'Winston, shut your fuckin' mouth and turn off that

junk music. How you 'spect to do this job if we come rollin' in like some fuckin' mobile disco!'

Winston turned off the radio with deliberate reluctance and looked suitably hurt.

'There, there it is.' Thomas pointed to a building on their left and Ziggy stopped the van and switched off the lights. By the side of the building was a loading bay and the front of the building was one large roller door with a small side door next to it.

'Reverse up there,' Thomas whispered. 'There are some windows on the side of the building.'

Ziggy reversed the old Transit into the loading bay and switched off. They sat quite still for a moment, listening to the silence. Thomas was the first out. He went to the lowest window in the side of the building, took a large roll of adhesive tape from his pocket and quietly tore it into lengths, sticking the strips over one of the windows.

'Are you sure dis is gonna work?' Winston's eyes bulged and he looked very nervous.

'You wanna go home, Winston?'

'No.'

'Well, what d'you think we should do then, ring on the fuckin' door?'

Winston said nothing and Thomas looked apprehensively at Ziggy. 'We should have left him at home. I told you.'

'Get on with it,' Ziggy said softly and handed Thomas a hammer wrapped in cloth. He looked about him and then gave the glass a sharp blow. Thirty seconds later Thomas was inside the building. He gave the surrounding area a quick inspection with his flashlight and opened the side door. Winston edged inside and nervously began to inspect the goods that were on shelves supported by metal racking. Thomas began to carry boxed video recorders to the open door and Ziggy took them from him and quietly loaded them into the van.

49

'Don't just stand there, man, get some stuff onto the truck. Hurry,' hissed Thomas.

Winston nodded and took the flashlight. He moved away from the aisle that Thomas was emptying and shone the light on the shelves at head height. There were boxes of hi-fi equipment, transistor radios and on a low shelf brown paper parcels. He took a parcel; it felt soft and he carried it out to the truck.

'What y'got there, Winston?'

'Dunno – let's see,' he said and ripped open the brown paper and discovered sweat-shirts. Ziggy threw them into the back of the truck.

'You stupid git, go and get something that's worth a bob or two – you ain't gonna get rich quick on sweatshirts,' and he pushed Winston back into the building.

Thomas was working methodically, moving two video recorders at a time, mentally keeping a note of the value of their night's work. He moved silently but by now was breathing hard and he stopped to catch his breath. He was pointing the flashlight down to read his watch when out of the darkness, behind his head, something hit him. The neck vertebrae snapped and his head fell limply to one side as he collapsed on the hard concrete floor. He lay motionless and the flashlight clattered on the floor and went out.

Winston, unaware of any danger, continued inspecting the contents of the shelves, and as his own flashlight swept past a gap in the shelves he saw a face. He froze and moved the light back to the gap in the shelving. The face was gone.

'Thomas.' He let out a hoarse whisper and shuddered. Suddenly he was very frightened. He followed the line of the shelves to the corner and then his foot struck something soft. He looked down and in the pool of light from his flashlight he saw the body of Thomas. His head bent back at an alarming angle, an arm caught beneath his body in a grotesque attitude and a thin trickle of blood oozing from his mouth.

50

'Ziggy!' He turned to run for the door but an arm hooked under his chin and held him still, vice-like, and suddenly all the fluorescent lights flickered and then, like instant daylight, came on.

Ziggy froze in the doorway and he saw Winston and his captor and at the top of a flight of stairs, a huge man with a beard.

'Get him!' bellowed the huge man, and then Ziggy moved. He leapt into the Transit, started the motor and drove like he'd never driven before; and as he turned the first corner, most of the stolen goods spewed out in a cascade of cardboard and polystyrene, slithering and tumbling across the road, then bursting open as they smashed into the kerb.

Davros was a Greek Cypriot, born in Limassol but had been in England since '62; he moved fast for a big man, and was quickly down the stairs.

'Has he got away?' He spoke with a thick accent, but his pronunciation was deliberate and very clear. Another man was at the doorway looking out into the night. He turned to face Davros and there was a blank look on his face. The man was a Korean. Davros repeated his question. 'Has he got away?' The man nodded and then closed the door.

Winston's eyes bulged with fear and with the pressure from the arm lock round his neck. The man who held him stood still and Davros turned them both like two dolls carved from the same block of wood. He nodded and then waved his hand at the man, who released Winston from his grip. Winston's head turned back to look at his captor. He too was Korean, the twin brother of the man at the door.

Suddenly there was a movement at the top of the stairs. She was dressed in black and wore a black hat with a veil covering her face. She stood for a moment on the landing then slowly, with a measured tread, descended. The heels of her shoes clacked and echoed across the floor until she stood in front of Winston. He

51

stood petrified as the face behind the veil looked at him.

'What have they taken?' she said.

Davros checked the shelves. 'Videos – I think that's all – about a dozen I would guess,' and then softly, almost to himself, 'one of the packets has gone.'

'Are you sure? Count them quickly.' She turned back to Winston. 'Did you take a packet of sweatshirts?'

Winston felt the back of his throat go dry as he tried to speak. 'Just one, miss,' he said, 'we took one. I'll get it back for you. Please don't hurt me – I'll get it back.'

Davros cupped Winston's face in his enormous hand. 'Where does the other one live?'

'I don't know.'

'You'd better remember or I'll snap your neck.'

Winston began to shake. 'Honest, I don't know – he has a stall in Brewer Street. His name is Ziggy, that's all I know. I swear on the book.'

'Hold him!' the woman said, and as the two Korean brothers took his arms, she withdrew a long pin from her hat. Winston watched the pin in total disbelief and as he looked back at the face behind the veil, she plunged the hat pin into his heart. He let out a soft gasp of surprised death and the two Koreans took his weight as his legs ceased to support him. She withdrew the pin, wiped a small amount of blood onto his collar and replaced it into her hat.

'Get Ziggy in the morning.' She spoke slowly to the two Koreans, who nodded together like matching oriental bookends and then she left, with Davros in her wake.

The Korean twins nodded to one another and silently went about the business of disposal.

Two hours later they had packed two dozen black plastic bags into the boot of the Silver Shadow, and after hosing down the concrete yard at the back of the building, they drove to a farm on the northern edge of Epping Forest. To the rear of the main farm buildings

52

was the dark, low silhouette of a large piggery and it was here that the Rolls-Royce came to discharge its cargo. Half an hour later, in the total silence of the air-conditioned walnut and leather interior, the two Koreans drove away from the farm and headed back to London. Outside shrill squeals of delight, punctuated by the guttural grunts of the Large Whites, rang long and loud on the edge of the forest and by dawn the last Caribbean morsel had been rooted from the farthest corner of the sty. Thomas and Winston had been converted.

Makepeace dug in up the hill to Jack Straw's Castle and The Spaniards, and as the ground levelled off she eased back and jogged past the old pub, through the archway and on down into Hampstead Village and her flat. The fine drizzle mingled with the beads of perspiration on her face and she wiped her forehead with the sweatband on her wrist. The last trace of hangover had been run off and she felt ready for a fresh start on a new calendar. She liked new things and as she slipped out of her sodden tracksuit and selected the clothes that she'd wear that day, she remembered her new partner.

She stood under the shower and let the perspiration wash off her body before she applied any soap or shampoo. The fine jets of water were warm and almost painful, and she stood still for some minutes wondering why she disliked Lootenant Dempsey so much, or if indeed it was actually the reverse. Maybe it was attraction to him and a dislike for herself – or maybe it was just plain nothing.

She washed quickly and changed into work clothes: jeans, white silk shirt and a soft, light grey leather jacket. She sat alone at the pine table in the kitchen, surrounded like a custodian, with the bric-à-brac of a marriage that was no more. She took the top off her solitary egg with practised indifference. It was quite raw. She went to the hob and felt the water that was still in the small pan. It was cold, as was the electric ring.

'Shit!' She hissed at her stupidity, threw the egg away and left.

The apartment that had been allocated to Dempsey was in Cannon Hill, off the Finchley Road; a large flat on the first floor of an old Victorian block called Marlborough Mansions. It was modestly and sparsely furnished but quite comfortable, and when the doorbell rang it echoed along the wide passageway to the bathroom at the end. Dempsey clambered out of the bath, wrapped a towel round his waist and took the ·44 Magnum from its holster that hung from a chair. He walked quietly down the passageway and listened by the side of the doorway, resisting the temptation to stand in front of the door. The memory of Joe Spitzer was still pretty clear in his mind. The bell rang again and he jumped at the coarse ring. There was nothing melodious about his house bell.

'Who is it?' he said casually.

'It's the Express Pizza Company – you wanna open up – or shall I push it under the door?'

Dempsey smiled, reapplied the safety catch to the Magnum and opened the door wide.

'Good morning, Sergeant Makepeace – come on in,' and he jerked the Magnum towards the kitchen. 'You want some coffee? I just made some fresh.'

Harriet Makepeace strolled past him, inspecting the flat as she went.

'Do you always bathe with that thing?' she said as she went into the kitchen and poured herself a cup of coffee. 'There's no need, you know. This is England, not America.'

'Lady – has anything I said to you yesterday registered or not?' He followed her into the kitchen. 'Whilst I admire your cavalier attitude – we better get a couple of things straight, or one of us is gonna wind up in the morgue. First off, whether this is London or New York,

54

the stakes for trafficking drugs are just as high – and if the stakes are high then little considerations about personal safety don't feature too highly in their rule book. Secondly, if you don't wise up to the fact that I am "numero uno" on just one of many hit lists, then I may as well not have a back-up person at all. Homicide to the mob, lady, is like clay-pigeon shooting to a hunter – it's just practice.'

Makepeace sipped her coffee indifferently.

'And thirdly?' she asked.

'Thirdly, I ain't ever worked with a dame before. I don't like female cops, ain't never met a good one yet, don't believe they exist.' She continued to sip her coffee.

'And do you always talk in unfinished, ungrammatical, staccato half-sentences, because if you do I think I shall have to invest in a phrase-book. Frankly, your use of the English language – the only thing we have in common – might just as well be Hindustani.' She put the cup of coffee down and looked him in the eye. 'Regarding the question of female competence, I would be obliged if you dismiss from your mind the fact that I'm a woman and just concentrate on getting on with the job. You never know, you might even learn something.'

Dempsey stood dripping water for a moment, then he scratched the side of his nose with the muzzle of the Magnum and grinned at Makepeace.

'Have it your way, honey – I'll just treat you like one of the boys – if that's the way you want it,' and he took off the towel and turned slowly before leaving the room. Makepeace tried not to watch his naked body saunter down the passage to his bedroom.

'Son-of-a-bitch,' she said under her breath, but she watched all the same.

Her old black Mini was parked outside the block, and ten minutes after the New York Nude Encounter, Dempsey and Makepeace stood on the pavement of Cannon Hill.

'Do we get a cab or what?' he asked, looking up and down the tree-lined road. He hunched his shoulders against the cold and looked at Makepeace.

She nodded towards the Mini and rattled the keys. 'The squad car awaits.'

'Squad car – this is yours?'

'Well, not exactly mine, it's the department's.'

Dempsey thrust his hands deeper into the pockets of his coat. 'This car belongs to the police?'

'Yes – don't you have unmarked cars in New York?'

'I guess so,' he said, 'but not like . . .' his voice trailed away. 'I suppose you're goin' to tell me that there's a souped-up Chevvy engine lurking under your hood.'

Makepeace opened the passenger door and ushered Dempsey in. 'No, not quite – in fact I think it's running a big-end bearing.' She slammed the door on Dempsey but it wouldn't shut until she'd turned round and given it what-for with her bottom. He closed his eyes as the car rocked slightly and didn't open them again until she'd got in on the driver's side.

'Will you fasten your seat-belt please?' she said rather formally.

He gave her an old-fashioned look. 'Is it really necessary?'

'It's the law,' she replied tartly and after three attempts, started the car.

For the first time in her life she drove very badly, and when they came to rest outside S.I.10 she was feeling decidedly tetchy and Dempsey had enough ammunition for a two-hour critique on the perils of driving with a woman.

He unbuckled his seat-belt and looked at her seriously. 'It's a good law, Makepeace. We should have the same law for women drivers in the States, too!'

Her response was succinct.

When they walked into the outer office of S.I.10, Spikings was rushing about like a dog with two dicks.

56

' 'arry!' he snapped, before they'd even sat down, 'come 'ere, and bring Wyatt Earp with you.'

They went into his office and he shut the door.

'Something's about to pop – I can feel it in me water.' He paced up and down and began to talk, almost as if he was alone. Makepeace sat and began to take notes. Dempsey just watched the manic perambulations of his new boss.

'. . . and the customs boys at Felixstowe seem pretty sure. Sure, but not certain. But those bastards are seldom wrong, and they've got a real sniff on this one.'

'So why didn't they pull the truck?' Makepeace asked.

'They did; went through it with a fine toothcomb. Ripped the bloody thing apart – and wound up with egg all over their face.'

'But they're still not convinced it was clean.'

Spikings shook his head. 'No, but they'd done so much damage to the truck and found nothing, they lost their bottle, stamped his ticket and let him through.'

'Did the driver complain?'

'Did he! Kicked up a hell of a fuss – but then he'd 'ave to. It'd look pretty rum if he just touched his cap and drove off with a truck in tatters, wouldn't it?'

'Did we put a tail on the truck?'

'As far as the North Circular.' Spikings rubbed his chin and looked out of the window.

'And then?' she said.

'The tail-car got a puncture, didn't it?'

'I don't believe it.' Makepeace felt embarrassment for the third time that morning, but Dempsey laughed softly.

'It happens,' he said. 'I was tailing a guy last year sometime and I was so goddamn keen not to lose him I ran clean outta gas in the middle of Bucks County.'

Makepeace smiled for the first time at her new partner – so he was human after all.

'So what did you do?' she asked with genuine interest.

'I said I'd gotten a puncture – what the hell else was I supposed to say.'

The telephone rang and interrupted the laughter. Spikings looked at them both. 'He's right here, Ed,' he said and handed the phone to Dempsey. 'It's your friend and mine – Ed Zukko. Things are about to hot up.'

Ed Zukko sat up in his bed; it was 03.30 in the New York Hilton and Ed was very tired. It had been one of those days.

'Dempsey – he took off from J.F.K. about ten minutes ago – the flight got screwed up with an engine out, so they've all been hanging around in a transit lounge for fuckin' hours. He's travelling under the name of Patterson and we've done the old toothpaste routine with him. Listen, Dempsey – are you sure you can handle this one? – it's important. Okay. Well, you'd better get your tail off to Heathrow when you've found out the ETA. He's flying Lufthansa – I don't know the number, but it's running about ten hours late so it won't be too hard to find out when it's due in. Is Gordon still there? Okay – put him on. Hi, Gordon – looks like the show's on the road, baby – keep me posted and tell Dempsey to take it easy – he's in pitching with the big boys.'

Spikings put the phone down and looked at Dempsey. 'Sounds like the honeymoon's over for you two, short and sweet, eh?'

Dempsey looked fondly at Makepeace and put a hand on her shoulder. 'Well, Makepeace old bean, they said it would never last, but this is ridiculous.'

She smiled at her whirlwind partner and stood up. 'I'll find out when the flight's due in and then we'll get down there and brief the customs people. Okay?'

'We'll all go together,' Spikings chipped in. 'If you'll pardon the intrusion.'

'Do I take it that means we go in your car, sir?'

Spikings nodded. 'May as well, Dempsey, I'll get it brought round.'

Dempsey breathed a sigh of relief and grinned at Makepeace, who left the office resisting the temptation to close the door with the panache of a seventh dan black belt.

As the weary passengers filed through the customs area at Terminal One, they were unaware of the observers behind the one-way glass of the customs observation section. Spikings, flanked by Dempsey and Makepeace, watched as the queue below them shuffled past the passport inspection desk.

'Seen 'im yet?' Spikings grunted to Dempsey.

'Nope.'

'You're sure you'll still recognize him?'

'Yep.'

Makepeace caught the attention of her boss and raised one eyebrow. 'Great conversationalist, isn't he, sir, in a monosyllabic sort of way.'

Spikings replied without looking at her. 'I'm not sure I don't prefer that to verbal diarrhoea, Makepeace, if you get my meaning.'

She turned away, but caught the grin that appeared on Dempsey's face, and in an uncharacteristic way she blushed and felt rather foolish.

'That's him,' Dempsey said, and all traces of the grin quickly disappeared from his face. He pointed down on to the floor of the customs area. 'The guy at the far end, in the camel coat and the grey fedora.'

'Are you sure?'

'As sure as a dead man stinks!' And he looked down at Schwartz and remembered the girl who'd died in the back of the chequer cab and he made a silent promise to himself.

The customs officer inspected the American passport casually, and then asked, 'Here on business, Mr Patterson?'

He smiled an innocent, welcoming smile. 'Business and pleasure – I like mixing both.'

'Quite so, sir. Have you anything other than the normal duty-free allowance, sir?'

'I don't even have that – what s the problem anyway?'

'Oh, no problem, sir, just a routine check, that's all. Would you mind just opening your suitcase, sir – shan't keep you long.' The customs man's smile widened as he turned the suitcase to face him. 'Is it locked, sir? Oh, thank you,' and he took the keys that were offered.

Spikings watched through the one-way glass, and listened to the conversation on the selective loudspeaker that was wired into each inspection point.

'Your friend's pretty cool, Dempsey, so far.'

'He's clean, he ain't got no cause to be otherwise – except for the false passport, that is.'

They watched as the customs man looked between the folded clothes. He took a brown leather toilet bag from the case and from the bag he removed a tube of toothpaste. His voice over the loudspeaker was tinged with just a hint of continued unconcern. 'This is your normal brand, Mr Patterson?'

'I guess – my secretary takes care of all those details.'

'I see, sir,' and he unscrewed the top of the toothpaste and squeezed. A fine trickle of white powder ran out into his palm.

'Well, well, sir – keen on decay is she, your secretary?'

'What's that? I don't understand.'

The man looked wildly about him.

'Heroin, Mr Patterson – or is it Schwartz?' He leant across the counter. 'Your feet aren't going to touch the ground, sunshine.'

Spiking turned to the uniformed Chief Inspector who stood to the rear of Dempsey and Makepeace. 'On no account must he be allowed to speak to anyone – no phone calls, no brief, nothing. Is that understood?'

60

'Yes, sir – but I don't know how long we can hold him.'

'For as long as I say. I don't care how loud he hollers, don't let 'im go, got it?'

The Chief Inspector nodded without much conviction.

'I mean it,' Spikings reaffirmed. 'If 'e gets let out, your head will roll. Is that crystal clear, Chief Inspector?'

Davros parked the Rolls outside the terminal building and went inside. He stood a little apart from the relatives and friends who were crowded along the barrier next to the exit from the passenger customs area. He watched the tired travellers as they came into the main terminal and looked for the people who were meeting them, like moles breaking ground for the first time, and then he saw the camel coat and grey fedora and he held up a rectangular card with the name 'Patterson' written in shaky capitals.

'Mr Patterson?' he said.

'The name's Schwartz – take my bag,' and Davros reluctantly took the bag and turned to the exit doors.

'This way,' he said sharply and he walked quickly to the waiting Rolls-Royce. He opened the rear passenger door before tossing the suitcase roughly into the boot.

'How nice to meet you, Mr Schwartz. My name is Merle,' and she nodded to Davros, who had taken up his position behind the wheel.

'Drive on, Davros. Mr Schwartz and I have a great deal to discuss.'

Dempsey took off the grey fedora and looked at Merle. 'Somebody just died?' He nodded at her veil.

'Oh yes – but then in our business death is always just around the next corner, don't you think?' and she lifted the veil from her face and Dempsey gaped for a moment at one of the most beautiful faces he'd ever seen.

Her cheekbones were very high and her eyes were

green and set wide apart. Beneath the small hat and veil her hair shone like polished jet and her mouth was red and full and gloss-wet.

'Why do you stare, Mr Schwartz?' Her voice was deep for a woman, and Dempsey felt a shudder of excitement run through his body.

'I beg your pardon, ma'am. I didn't think I was gonna be working with such a good-looking dame, that's all. I'll try not to stare, okay?'

She smiled at him and touched his knee. 'Mr Schwartz, when the deal is done you can look all you want – until then let's just keep it business. Okay?' and she lowered her veil. The Rolls drove away, followed by two black cabs and an unmarked van.

Spikings watched the vehicles leave the forecourt in front of the terminal building and then he turned to Makepeace. 'Well, 'arry. So far so good. Shall we go?'

She looked up at the Chief Inspector like a daughter would look at her father. 'D'you think he'll be all right?'

Spikings shrugged. 'Don't know, gal – we'll just have to keep our fingers crossed. Anyway – thought you didn't like him.'

She wrinkled up her nose and looked after the Rolls. 'He's all right. I think.'

CHAPTER FIVE

Jimmy-le-Bone was the shoeshine on Westminster Bridge. He also played trombone to West End queues in the evening, lived rough and drank like only a Glaswegian can; like he had shares in Johnny Walker and he, personally, was responsible for their profitability. Jimmy was also a snout for Harriet Makepeace, and a good one. There wasn't much that Jimmy didn't know about in the 'smoke', and he earned well out of it. Fifty a week, on most weeks, and sometimes more, but his information, although always kosher, usually left Makepeace with a lot of leg work and a lot more questions left unanswered. When she got back to S.I.10 with Spikings, there was a message from Jimmy – he wanted a meet.

She drove to the Elephant and then on to Westminster Bridge. She crossed the bridge and spotting Jimmy sat outside the underground entrance, parked the Mini round the back of Old Scotland Yard's building in Cannon Place. She sat in the chair and Jimmy began to apply oxblood polish to her boots. He finished the first boot before he spoke, and he talked without looking up from his task.

'Are them boots Italian?'

'Yes,' she said. 'What news today, Jimmy? Make it quick, I really shouldn't be here,' and she looked up at Big Ben and checked her watch.

'Ziggy wants a word.'

'Ziggy? I haven't seen him for months.'

'Wants to see you's. In a bit of bother I think. Might be worth you having a chat, y'know what I mean?'

'Is he still on his stall?'

'Aye, but he's shit scared.' He finished the second boot and looked up at Makepeace. The purple veins on his nose looked more like a map of the underground, due in part to the cold weather, but more particularly to a hogmanay that would have brought about a cardiac arrest in anyone but a Clydesdale or Jimmy, and he had two front teeth missing.

'What happened to the teeth, Jimmy?'

He grinned broadly, not a pretty sight at the best of times, but with two fresh, bloody roots showing in the bottom gum it guaranteed nausea at best, projectile vomiting at worst.

'I was doing the queue outside the old Windmill, s'got a fresh name now, and some o'them punk bastards tried to shove the fuckin' trombone down m'throat.'

'Looks like they damned nearly succeeded.' She passed him a tenner and got up. 'Your information, as usual, Jimmy, on face value seems worthless. But you do have an annoying habit of nearly always pointing me in an interesting direction.' She paused before walking back to her car. 'I know it's wasted breath, but I'd see a dentist if I were you.'

He laughed like an old hyena, and wiped his mouth with the cuff of his sleeve. Traces of blood and saliva glistened on the rough jacket material like the trail of a mortally wounded snail and he waved at Makepeace.

'If I get enough grog inside me of an evening, I feel no pain, lassie, not until the morning anyhow, and you don't need teeth for drinking.' He slipped the ten pound note in his top pocket and winked at her. 'You go and see Ziggy – before he gets out of his depth.'

She promised that she would and waved farewell to Jimmy-le-Bone as she turned the corner and returned to her car which was about to receive first prize for double yellow parking.

'Sorry – must dash,' she said, flipped her identity card casually from her back pocket and smiled sweetly at the fat female traffic warden.

The Mini started first time and Makepeace drove away, leaving the traffic warden poised with her expensive little plastic parcel and a mouthful of language heavy with verbal cholesterol. She drove down Whitehall until the traffic ground to a halt and then jostled its way slowly round Trafalgar Square, like hundreds of privately owned dodgem cars reversing the reflexes of a lifetime and playing the avoiding game. She felt depressed as the traffic silently jockeyed for position, and in that grey January she missed the heat and clamour and social whirl of the British Embassy in Rome.

For six years her father had been in the diplomatic service, and had run the British Embassy in Rome rather more on the lines of a club in St James's. She'd lost her heart to Rome at an early age, and her virginity, and although her sense of patriotism, fair play and loyalty to the Crown would probably always prevent her from pulling the plug on the old country, there was part of her that yearned for la dolce vita. The Latin streak in Dempsey seemed to be one of his few redeeming features, and as the traffic continued on its polite, sluggish way around Nelson's Column, she worried about whether he was still in one piece with the black widow and the huge Greek, and she wondered what on earth Ziggy wanted.

From the fifth floor in Grosvenor Place it's possible to see almost all the gardens of Buckingham Palace and in the summer, in the Royal Garden Party season, the queues of guests that keep Moss Bros. in business, can be seen perambulating and shuffling like king penguins, parading themselves in front of their queen. In winter, however, it looks much like any formal garden or park, all greens and browns.

Lei Shan looked down from her window and for a moment felt the cold thrill of revenge pass through her body. She replaced the receiver and stared at the Royal backgarden with a wistful, faraway look in her almond eyes. Her finger nails were long and they touched the keys on the telephone. It was like the precise peckings

65

of a maribou on the dead carcass of a wildebeest. She held the handset close to her ear, and spoke softly as her call was answered.

'Hello – is that Oriental Banking and Finance? Could I speak to Sir Charles Kershaw, please. No, it's a personal call – thank you.' She sat back and waited for the president of the bank to reply.

'Sir Charles? It's Lei Shan.' She paused. 'I'm collecting for Poppy Day. Yes, he's arrived from the States. No, but I'm sure he'll be in touch as soon as possible. Sir Charles, will you let me know when the funds are available – if what I know of Schwartz is true, he'll want to get in and out as quickly as possible.' She nodded at his reply and replaced the telephone as if her mind was on the other side of the world.

She pushed the telephone away and turned her swivel chair through ninety degrees so she could put information on a keyboard and VDU. The screen leapt into life and massed an army of green numbers onto its greyness. She tapped out more figures with her stork-like fingers, watched them reform and as the mathematical space-invaders brought about a final calculation she made some notes from the screen full of figures and then 'dumped' the entire floppy disk into oblivion – posterity wouldn't understand.

There was a knock on the door and automatically she put her figures into the top drawer of the desk and locked it.

'Come.' Her voice was without emotion, almost formal.

The door opened and a man came into the office. He was fortyish and looked mid-European, from Turkey or maybe Albania, and there was a tell-tale bulge under his left armpit telegraphing to those that know of those things, that he was carrying a gun. His name was Serge and he was not only her private secretary, but also her minder.

'You wish to see me?' His voice was low and humble,

almost servile, and he resisted the temptation to bow in the presence of his beautiful employer, for whom he would, quite willingly, lay down his life.

'Yes, Serge – the negotiator from New York has arrived. He was met at Heathrow this morning by the big Greek and the woman.'

'Who is he – do we know of him?'

'Yes – his name is Schwartz; he is ex-CIA.'

'Ex-CIA? There is never such a thing – should we check him out?'

Lei Shan shook her head and looked out again into the gardens below, and once again her eyes glazed with the bitterness of a bad memory.

'No – that won't be necessary, but afterwards we need to make some arrangements.'

'Permanent arrangements?'

'Oh, yes, Serge – most permanent,' and for a moment she lapsed into silence. 'My grandfather was a senior aide to Chiang Kai-Shek, and when he died our family moved to Burma and then to Laos. The man Schwartz was involved in flying and supplying opium to the new government troops in Laos; our village was the handover point.'

'The CIA supplied it?' His question had the innocent ring of a child.

'Oh yes – many times, many times.' And once again she drifted off into her memory bank. 'There was a day I shall never forget, the day my mother was taken from our house by a Burmese officer who had come to do business with Schwartz. They took her and raped her,' she stared out of the window, 'many times, until she could no longer walk.'

'Why did they take her, what had she done?'

Lei Shan laughed in order to prevent herself from crying. 'Because her father had worked with Chiang Kai-Shek, because it was Tuesday,' she shrugged, 'because they wanted a woman – who knows. After they had finished with her they tied her hands and dragged her through the village behind a jeep, until she was dead.' She paused again. 'And when we asked for her body, they refused. They said it was to be left for the wild animals to eat – a fitting end, they said, for all the Kuomintang,' and her eyes brimmed with grief.

Serge approached cautiously and laid a hand on her shoulders. 'This Schwartz man – he was one of them?'

She looked up at him and touched his hand. 'He drove the jeep.'

The Rolls-Royce stopped outside a large white Regency house in Hanover Terrace. Davros got out of the car and went round to open the rear door for Merle, but Dempsey had already got out and was offering Merle his hand. She took advantage of the offer much to the chagrin of Davros, and Dempsey nodded to him, grinned and said, 'Don't forget my suitcase, buster,' turned his back on him and took Merle by the arm.

'Is this home? Looks pretty ritzy.'

She raised her veil for the second time that day, and smiled at him. 'The inside is even ritzier – come, I have some phone calls to make. Davros will show you your room and after you've freshened up we'll go and see the stuff before it gets processed.'

'I'd like that,' and he escorted her up the path to the front door. Davros followed with the suitcase and as Dempsey closed the front door he nodded imperceptibly to the man in a tracksuit, who jogged past the Rolls-Royce. It was Morris.

The door closed and Morris pressed the remote switch in the palm of his hand that operated the throat microphone.

'Hello, Charlie three. He's gone into No. 4 Hanover Terrace with the woman in black and the gorilla – I'll hang about. Over.' He jogged on and listened to the dulcet tones of Spikings in an earpiece that only he could hear.

'Charlie Three – be very careful – we're on bloody thin ice; one slip and Dempsey'll be up to his neck in it. Over.'

'Charlie Three, Roger out,' and he crossed the road and ran back past the house.

Makepeace parked on a meter in Wardour Street, more out of guilt than luck, and made her way to Berwick Street. She picked her way through the stalls of questionable Christmas fruit and cheap boxed presents, some of which she knew to be nicked. Some of the stallholders nodded as she passed and a couple called out to her and waved. Halfway down on the left she saw Ziggy. He sat on the edge of his stall and swayed in rhythm to the inevitable reggae that came over the cheap plastic earphones that protected his ears from the cold, but not from the decibels.

She tapped him on the shoulder after two verbal attempts at communication failed. He spun round in surprise and almost fell off the stall. His eyes were wide and Makepeace knew Ziggy had been at the juice. He took off the earphones and she could hear the music from where she stood.

'Jimmy-le-Bone said you wanted to see me. So make it quick because I'm not supposed to be here.'

He brushed his hand across his nose; it moved as though it wasn't attached to anything in particular, and he looked up and down the street like a scared rabbit.

'We did a job last night.'

'Should you be telling me this, Ziggy?'

'It was up Wembley – the old industrial estate, behind de Stadium.'

'Go on.'

'We got jumped and me two mates got nobbled. I was driving de truck so I got meself away, but I had to leave de other two in de shit.'

'Survival of the fastest, I suppose,' but the sarcasm was wasted on Ziggy.

'But de thing is – I ain't see de other two at all.'

Makepeace wasn't impressed. 'Ziggy – I've driven half across London to come and see you, and all you've got is some half-baked story about some tuppenny-ha'penny blag that backfired that you were part of . . .'

'I think one of me mates was hurt – he was lying on de ground – and nobody knows where they are.'

'Well, I would imagine they're safe and sound in the bosom of Ealing nick, wouldn't you?'

Ziggy gave Makepeace an old-fashioned look. 'Do us a favour – they won't be in no nick. All de stuff in de warehouse was off de back of a truck. What d'you tink dey're gonna do – report to de fuzz dat deir stolen property's stolen?'

'Well, what did you nick?'

'Videos mainly, and most of them went out de back of de truck when I moved off.'

'So no-one in their right mind is going to run the risk of going down for GBH over a few videos now, are they, Ziggy? Be reasonable.' She looked at her watch. 'Give me the address – I'll check it out, but I really think your concern for your comrades, touching as it may be, is uncalled for.'

He gave her the address, and as she was about to leave she saw a pile of sweatshirts on his stall.

'Where d'you get these from, Ziggy?' She held one up against her. It was white and across the chest in black lettering were the words 'Make peace not war'.

Ziggy grinned. 'Shit, man, I forgot all about dem – you can have one on de house. Compliments of de management.' He nodded at the garment, 'It's got your moniker on it.'

She folded it over her arm and began to walk away. 'I'll let you know about your mates – but, please, don't involve me again in any more of your own business, just tell me about the good stuff. So long, Ziggy,' and she disappeared into the crowd. Ziggy looked after her and then replaced the headphones and relaxed again into the temporary oblivion of Jimi Hendrix.

He didn't hear the two Koreans behind him and no-one noticed the pressure grip applied to his carotid

70

artery. The two Koreans had been gone for over a quarter of an hour before an old lady accidentally nudged Ziggy in passing and sent him sprawling into the gutter and the discarded Christmas fruit. Jimi Hendrix had been playing to dead ears for fifteen minutes or more.

Makepeace spoke to the big black who gave the change and kicked out the drunks at the Pink Pussycat Peep Show.

'Is Gloria working today?'

'Who wants to know?' he replied suspiciously.

'A friend.'

'You looking for a job?'

'Not exactly. Is she here?'

The big black shrugged indifferently. 'Take a look, I got all the change you want, lady.'

Makepeace gave the man a crisp pound note and he fished into a filthy cloth pocket that hung around his belly, like a kangaroo's pouch that had seen better days. Makepeace took the two fifty-pence pieces as though they were carriers of yellow fever and paused, half expecting a swarm of blow-flies to escape from the sagging sack of change that the man constantly ran his stubby fingers through, in absent-minded pleasure.

The two coins felt warm in her hand, and she shuddered slightly as she went into a cubicle on the left side of two rows of similar cubicles, that faced each other like a badly lit ladies' lavatory. She locked the door behind her and put a coin into the slot in the facing wall. Behind the wall, which seemed to be made of hardboard painted with dark brown emulsion paint and stained a lot at waist level, she heard the familiar crutch-grinding music of the strippers' world, and as the coin dropped in the box a flap lifted on the letter-box-sized slit and she looked in.

There were maybe eight or nine cubicles on three sides of a square, and Makepeace could see men's unblinking eyes on either side staring through their

71

own little rectangles of fantasy at the girl in front of them. There was a chipped, bent-wood chair in the middle of the floor and behind the girl a large, cracked mirror. The girl was bending over the chair, cupping a pair of extremely tired tits in nicotine-stained hands and swaying in time with the scratching music. She had her back to the mirror and as she slowly opened her legs to straddle the chair, Makepeace wondered if the eyes behind the slits were on the mirror or the girl. She looked at the girl's face and saw the hopeless, unseeing glaze on her eyes as she stared up at the black ceiling and performed her excruciatingly ugly ritual. Her hair had once been blonde, but now little was left and the mousy roots were surfacing from her lousy scalp like lug worms on a doll's head. Her body looked grey and unwashed and there was an old purple scar on her belly in memory of her Caesarean still-born; even her pubic hair looked in need of a comb. Makepeace closed her eyes and leant on the wall. She felt sick.

When she opened her eyes again the girl was moving around the edge of the floor, performing, as if privately, to each open flap. Touching her matted crutch and rubbing her sagging breasts as though she was kneading dough, and talking to the eyes.

The flap on Makepeace's peep-hole closed with a creak and she hurriedly fumbled for the other coin. The flap obediently lifted on the strange set which only weeks before had been a hard-porn cinema, and Makepeace wondered how long the Pink Pussycat Peep Show would run. As long as it took Westminster Council to plug yet another loophole in the obscenity law, and then overnight the neon sign would re-phrase itself and the pathetic punters would continue to jerk themselves off in the hardboard cubicles of the mob. Only small change, but lots of it.

'D'you want a private show downstairs, luv? Ten pounds short time with a rubber, fifteen the full service with French.' The girl avoided the eyes in the darkness and looked blankly at the wall, somewhere above Makepeace's head.

'I'm looking for Gloria – does she still work here?'

The girl looked down at the slit and blinked at the couth female voice.

'Who are you?'

'A friend – I just want to talk with her.'

'She's working in the Taboo in Old Compton Street, she's stopped this game – gone all fuckin' la-di-da,' and she moved away and talked to the next opening. Makepeace watched her in the mirror as she said her lines to the next private audience, and she heard the acceptance of the proposition through the hardboard and she saw the girl leave the room through a curtained door. Loopholes within loopholes.

The man in the next cubicle left for the basement as Makepeace closed her cubicle door. He was fat, florid and wore a pinstripe suit and Makepeace thought that if he had a particularly rough channel crossing, his blood pressure would go off the dial. She nodded to him as he stared at her.

'If I were you I'd insist on her going through a sheep-dip first,' she said and left for the Taboo. The fat man hesitated for an instant and then scurried off in the direction of Shepherd Market; the girls were more expensive, but cleaner and the walk would do him good. He chuckled to himself as he hurried along Piccadilly. 'Sheep-dip, Shepherd Market,' he said aloud, and people looked at him condescendingly, as people do to mild eccentrics in London.

The Taboo Club was a down-market clip joint specializing in topless waitresses who should have known better, either because their sheer size prevented them from dispensing drinks with any degree of safety, or because their colour was so much in sympathy with the very low electricity bill that all that was visible was a set of teeth. Makepeace reluctantly paid up her three pounds entrance fee, which covered temporary club membership, and descended to the inevitable basement. Slowly her eyes adjusted to the darkness and she saw a knot of half-clad horrors perched around a small bar, like naked vultures, waiting silently for a fresh carcass to stumble in off the street.

Makepeace saw Gloria sitting with a man. He was watching an out-of-focus hard porn German movie that flickered on a dirty screen. There was a large blonde girl doing things to a donkey that hadn't appeared in any of the equestrian handbooks that Makepeace had read as a girl. She touched Gloria on the shoulder.

'Hello, luv, thought it wouldn't take you long to find me. 'Ow are you?'

'Can you tear yourself away from your stable companion for a few minutes – I want a word,' and she moved to the other side of the dark room and sat at a vacant table.

'D'you wanna drink?' Gloria said as she joined Makepeace.

'Not at your prices I don't.'

'On the 'ouse – what'll it be?'

'I'll have a glass of port – if they've got it.'

'Okay, Duchess – coming up,' and she went up to the bar, ordered a port for Makepeace and an orange juice for herself and came back to the table.

'What's up, 'arry?'

'I don't know. Jimmy-le-Bone told me this morning that Ziggy was in a panic. Ziggy said he'd been disturbed with his fingers in the till at a warehouse up at Wembley last night and was worried about two of his mates who, with typical Ziggy gallantry, he left in the shit. I saw him just now and he seems pretty concerned about their safety.' She paused as the donkey's indiscretion got the better of him, and then she continued. 'I just wondered if you'd heard anything that might save me a trip up to Wembley.'

A girl reluctantly waddled over with the drinks and put them down with such indifference that most of

Makepeace's port slopped off the table top and onto her silk shirt.

'Oh. Sorry,' she said. 'Will it wash out?'

Makepeace looked up at the girl with obvious distaste. 'Probably not,' she said flatly. 'Why – do you intend to do anything about it?'

The girl was without any apology and shrugged. 'I said sorry, what else d'you expect?'

Gloria waved the girl away. 'Oh, 'arry – I'm sorry. I should 'ave got 'em. Come through the back, you can borrow something of mine. I'll get it dry cleaned for you.' She felt the shirt. 'Silk ain't it?'

' 'Fraid so – lead on,' and she stood up and followed Gloria into a small room at the back which served as the girl's dressing room.

'Here – try this on,' and Gloria held up a scarlet Lurex jumper. Makepeace took the cheap garment and felt the coarseness of the knit, and handed it back to Gloria.

'It's all right – I've got this thing that Ziggy gave me. It'll do until I get home. But I will take you up on your offer to clean this.'

Gloria watched as Makepeace casually slipped out of the silk shirt, and she envied the fullness and the firmness of Makepeace's breasts.

'You'll never be outta work with tits like that, gal,' she said. Makepeace grinned, pulled the sweatshirt over her head and flicked her hair free with both hands.

'Don't you wear a bra then?' Gloria asked curiously. 'I thought your sort always did.'

Makepeace laughed. 'Very rarely – why, don't tell me you do.'

'When I leave here I do – you know, in case I 'ave an accident and 'ave to go to hospital. Got to 'ave a bra, haven't you? It's only right.'

CHAPTER SIX

The day was fading fast over North London, and by the time Makepeace had found the address that Ziggy had given her, most of the traffic was driving with lights. She saw the warehouse of *Action Video* as she drove slowly through the industrial estate behind Wembley Stadium. The large roller door was open and a truck was parked outside. Inside the warehouse the lights were on but the place seemed deserted. She parked the Mini and sat watching for any movement from within, but there was none. She reached for the radio handset and called into base.

'Hello Charlie two – can you check if last night there was a reported break-in at a video company in Wembley. Over.' Her call was acknowledged and she sat for some ten minutes before the reply came back.

'Hello Charlie two – negative. No reports of any sort last night in that area. I've checked with three nicks and none of 'em took any house guests last night. Over.'

She sat in the car for a couple of minutes more, and then decided to take a look. There was still no sign of movement from the warehouse and as the darkness descended, the brightly lit interior looked almost inviting. She got out of her car and walked the fifty yards to the open front of the warehouse, and as she stepped inside she remembered that she'd left the keys of her Mini in the ignition.

'Oh shit,' she said aloud, and turned to go back to her car.

'Yes? Can we help you?' The voice from the top of the stairs that led up to the office was very deep and very precise. Makepeace turned and looked up at Davros, Merle and behind her, Dempsey. Makepeace

76

remained unblinking, and her casual outward calm belied her internal panic as she looked up and smiled at the three of them. She parted her leather jacket at the waist, placed her hands on her hips and grinned even more. Her nerve had nearly gone and she was resisting the temptation to simply run away.

'Terribly sorry to trouble you, but I'm looking for the deep freeze people who make the foil containers for the fast food business. I saw them on the main notice board at the entrance to the estate – but I've been round twice and I still can't find them.' She stood still after her speech which, had it not been for one glaring error, would have been perfectly satisfactory; she would have been redirected and nothing more would have been said.

Dempsey held his breath and tried as hard as he could to remain impassive.

Merle looked back at Dempsey. 'Do you see what she's wearing?' she said in a low voice, 'it's one of our bloody shirts.'

Dempsey nodded and tried to look concerned. 'I guess it could be coincidence,' he said, but Merle was not convinced.

'Coincidence my arse,' and as if it was their cue, the two Koreans stepped from behind a row of shelving. One of them hit the button on the wall that operated the big roller door.

Makepeace spun as the roller door began to drop and saw the two Koreans closing in on her. The high-pitched whine of the electric motor sounded very loud and the metal slats of the unrolling door rattled as the door descended.

Davros waved an arm at the two Koreans and shouted at them. 'Get her!'

They looked up at him, unblinking and obedient, and then they looked at Makepeace. Dempsey's hand went to the Magnum that he carried in a shoulder holster, but he was uncertain of his next move.

They came at her slowly, confidently at first, but as

she read the situation, she dropped into a low crouch and when the first Korean came within range, she kicked and turned to face the other. The kick was a good one, and her polished Italian boots left an expensive Gucci impression. He staggered back, dropping to one knee and clutched at his shattered nose. The other one lunged at her and, as he made contact, she let herself fall back, pulling him with her and using his own forward momentum, she threw him rather convincingly into the metal shelving, which toppled and then fell, bringing the whole row down with it, like a pack of cards. She looked behind her and seeing the roller door nearly fully down, she ran and dived at the twelve inch gap, and wriggled under it and was gone before the roller door closed with a resounding clunk.

Dempsey turned to Merle. 'Well, I'm impressed.'

She disregarded the remark and began snapping orders. 'Get that door up – and get after her.'

Davros was halfway down the stairs and Dempsey followed. Behind him he heard the clack of Merle's shoes on the metal treads of the stairs, and as they got to the floor of the warehouse the roller door was already opening.

'Quickly, after her!' Merle screeched at the two Koreans as they peered out under the slowly ascending door.

Two more inches and they squeezed out and as they did, Dempsey heard the Mini failing to start. He followed the Koreans under the door out into the chill darkness of evening and saw them closing on the Mini. Makepeace was stabbing at the accelerator in an attempt to kick the thing into life, and with only seconds to spare, the engine caught and she moved away. Slowly at first, desperate lest she stall the car, and then as the first Korean was within a yard of the door handle, she gave the Mini all she'd got.

Dempsey stood still and watched powerless as the first of the two men closed on the car, and as the roller door continued to open, Davros bent with difficulty and then joined Dempsey.

Slowly, painfully, the Mini accelerated, and the Koreans were left panting in the road.

'Get after her, Davros – stop her at all costs, whoever she is, she'll go to the police – kill her, Davros!'

Davros now moved with great speed, and ran to the Rolls which was parked in the loading bay. Dempsey looked at Merle, and tapped at the bulge under his jacket. 'I'll keep him company.'

Merle nodded. 'There's a rifle in the car – use it.' He nodded, ran to the car and got into the passenger seat. Davros started the big seven-litre engine, and gave it the gun. The rear wheels spun and left rubber on the road, and the car leapt forward, uncharacteristically, and swung left after the disappearing tail-lights of Makepeace and her Mini.

She looked in her mirror and saw the headlights of the big Rolls stab into the darkness. She knew that unless she could give it the slip there was no way she'd outrun it.

The duty radio operator shouted to Spikings as the first transmission came in from Makepeace.

'Sir – Harry's in trouble!'

Spikings came from his office at the double, and grabbed the radio handset. 'Where is she?'

'She's up Wembley way, there's a unit in the area, sir, tailing Dempsey.'

'Dempsey? Is he on the move again?'

'Yes, sir.' The radio operator scratched his head. 'It seems that Dempsey and that Greek bloke are chasing her, sir.'

'Chasing who?'

'Harry, sir.'

Spikings frowned at the man and then spoke into the handset. 'Hello Charlie five – what's going on? Over?'

Makepeace grabbed at her radio mike as she dropped

the Mini into second and accelerated out of a round-about, changed up into third and then yelled into her handset.

'Charlie five – Christ knows – I saw one of my snouts earlier this afternoon – he was involved in a minor bit of tea-leafing last night. In a warehouse in Wembley. They got jumped when they were loading some videos into their van and he drove off. He said he was concerned about the safety of his mates who got left behind and asked me to check it out. Hang on.' She put the handset down and nipped between a bus and a container truck, and then turned left.

The Rolls braked hard to allow the bus to pass on its nearside, and then Davros swung the wheel and followed the Mini. Dempsey sat in the front and resisted the temptation to take the big Greek out. It would be so simple, but it wouldn't achieve a whole lot, Ed Zukko's operation would open like a can of worms and Dempsey would be about as popular as a pork chop in a synagogue.

Two cars behind the Rolls an old 1962 MkII Jaguar followed with an almost casual ease. The two men from S.I.10 watched the evasive action of Makepeace and the driver kept a respectable distance between the Jaguar and the Rolls. His mate sat back knowing that if it was necessary the old Jag would leave most things on the road standing, and if things got too hairy up front they could be up with them in seconds.

'Hello Charlie four, 'arry's trying 'er best to lose the Roller, but that Mini of 'ers 'as got less poke in it than a milk float. We'll intercept 'em if we 'ave to, but it's going to be a bit awkward like, with old Dempsey stuck in the middle like the jam in a sandwich,' and then he looked in the passengers' rear-view mirror and blew out a long column of smoke, stubbing out his cigarette.

'Shit, talking of jam sandwiches – we've got one up our bleedin' exhaust,' and he turned in his seat and looked out of the rear window. His mate looked in his mirror and swore under his breath as he saw the white Ford Granada with the red stripe down the side.

'It's the fuckin' law. Why do they always turn up at the wrong fuckin' time!' and he grabbed the handset from his mate.

'Hello Charlie four – we've got company, picked up a jam jar that looks like it's gonna pull us. Advise. Over.'

Spikings rubbed his short grey hair and closed his eyes for an instant.

'Hello Charlie four – lead them away; don't get the bloody woodentops involved for Christ's sake. I'll try and get another unit to pick up from you. Out to you. Hello Charlie five, how y'doing gal?'

Makepeace was watching the Rolls-Royce getting closer, and try as she might to cut quickly through the busy evening traffic, she seemed unable to lose the big car, which just seemed to appear larger and more stately in her mirror. Her mind was in a whirl, and she didn't really know where she was going or how she was going to try and extract herself from this crazy situation, until the question was asked by Spikings on the radio.

' 'arry, where are you making for? If you know that is, 'cos if you do perhaps I can send some of the boys there to hang about. Over.'

'Hello Charlie five – I'm going home. Over.'

Dempsey's feet were braced on the floor of the Rolls as it powered after the small Mini. Davros was good and he knew how to gain ground in traffic, and Dempsey watched as his big slug-like fingers twirled the steering wheel like a majorette twirling a baton. He too had noticed the police car following the S.I.10 Jaguar. He'd seen the Jag suddenly shoot off to the left, closely followed by the police car, and he'd assumed that he'd been told to get the hell out of it by Spikings. Davros had seen none of this, such was his concentration on the small Mini – but nonetheless Dempsey felt as though the last contact with the home team had been withdrawn; as though the plug had been pulled. He sat back and tried to appear an eager party in the chase, but his mind was racing with all the possible combinations and permutations. But try as he might he couldn't help feeling that sooner or later he was just going to have to blow out the Greek bastard's brains, because at every street and every turn they were gaining on the scurrying little car, and he imagined his new partner fighting with the wheel in order to make her car, which was so badly out of condition, perform like Paddy Hopkirk on a R.A.C. Rally.

Spikings had taken to the road and had mobilized all the possible S.I.10 units to proceed to the Hampstead area and lie low. He had a feeling that the spot his little female protegée was in was getting tighter, and he had absolutely no idea how Dempsey was going to play it. He sat in the back of his car oblivious to the risks his driver was taking. The whole unit was on maximum alert and all personally involved. One of them was in danger – and the bond between them all was far stronger than normal. They were all special in S.I.10, that's why they were there, and an élite organization always bust a gut to take care of its own, especially when the one in danger was a woman.

In all, six cars were converging fast on Hampstead and in each car, while the driver was concentrating on driving fast in traffic, his partner was checking out weapons and keeping Spikings briefed on their progress, and as they all got closer to the inevitable point of contact, so the uncertainty increased.

The Rolls was nearly up on the Mini when it turned sharply to the right, parked and Makepeace leapt out of the car and made a dash for the front door of her flat. Only seconds later the Rolls followed and Davros saw Makepeace as she disappeared into her apartment. He stopped the car and for the first time since the chase began, there was silence, apart from his heavy breathing.

He looked at Dempsey. 'The bird has flown home to her nest.'

Dempsey nodded and wondered what on earth the next move should be, but before he could answer, Davros reached behind the front seat and produced a .38 Tikka hunting rifle, which was hidden in a small compartment beneath the passenger seat.

'Here,' he said, 'go and finish her – the weapon is almost silent,' and he thrust the rifle into Dempsey's hands.

He took it and opened the breech. It was loaded. He looked tentative and Davros reacted with suspicion.

'What is wrong? The girl must be killed.'

'You bet your sweet ass! But I wanna check with Merle first.'

Davros looked at him strangely. 'What do you mean?'

Dempsey rounded on him. 'I mean, I wanna speak to Merle, you Greek asshole! What's her number?'

'Why?'

'Listen buster – the less you know the better – just gimme the number and I'll go down the road to the nearest call box and speak to her – okay?'

Davros looked confused. 'But . . .'

'Listen wise guy – who knows who this broad is. Maybe the smartest thing right now is to take her some place – maybe it's a dumb move to go and blow her away. Merle looks like a cute operator so let's ask her again – okay?' He jerked his thumb at Makepeace's flat. 'She ain't going no place.'

Davros shrugged and gave Dempsey the telephone number of the warehouse. He repeated it twice and then slipped away from the Rolls-Royce with his heart beating furiously.

At the bottom of the road was a telephone box and he opened the door, placed a hand on the shoulder of the woman talking to her sister, and said, 'Excuse me lady – this is kinda vital,' and eased her out of the box and dialled a memorized telephone number. The woman stood outside the box outraged at the interruption, but feeling unable to do anything that would significantly change the situation. Dempsey's determination was very apparent. He waited for a second, fumbled with some change, and then the ringing tone stopped and the urgent sound of the pips began. He pushed some small change into the appropriate slot and heard the connection.

'Hello,' he said, and smiled when he heard the reply.

When Makepeace closed the door of her flat she was out of breath, and she was still panting when she picked up the telephone.

'Hello,' she said, 'you must stop following me – people will begin to talk.'

'Very funny!'

'Are you supposed to be trying to kill me?'

'Yup.'

'Oh,' she paused, 'and are you?'

'Nope.'

'Oh good – I am glad. I thought, just for a moment, that you'd got quite carried away with the excitement of the chase,' and then more seriously, 'listen, what the fuck are we going to do – this is a ridiculous situation.'

Dempsey nodded. 'You can say that again baby.'

'Well – what are you going to do?'

There was a short silence, and then Dempsey said, 'I gotta idea.'

Davros was beginning to get twitchy, as he sat in the Rolls waiting for Dempsey to return. He watched the front door of Makepeace's flat like a hawk, unaware that two of the cars that had been parked in the street when they arrived belonged to S.I.10, and that during the time he'd been parked a further four had arrived and were either stationary or cruising the block. Spikings could see the Rolls from where he sat and he watched nervously as Dempsey walked back from the telephone box and got into the rear of the car.

'Hello, all stations Charlie,' his voice was very dry – and sounded somehow odd to all the units of S.I.10 waiting for some indication of what was likely to happen. It was very quiet and as Spikings continued to speak over the radio, it started to rain.

'. . . so I don't want any heroics from anyone. Just sit tight and as they say on the other side of the water, stay loose. Over and out.'

Dempsey sat very still and watched the doorway, and he knew that the longer they waited the more his credibility would slip as far as Davros was concerned.

The big man spoke softly, 'We must go in and get the girl – it is foolish to sit here – she may already have slipped away.'

But as he spoke the door opened a fraction and Dempsey tensed and slid the bolt forward on the Tikka rifle and eased a round into the breech.

'I don't think so – look,' and he pressed the switch that lowered the passenger door window. The rain from outside blew into the car and he felt the cold droplets of moisture on his face. He raised the stock of the rifle to his cheek and picked up the white door in the telescopic sight. Davros was nervous now, and Dempsey placed a hand on his shoulder.

'Start the car, Davros, and be ready to move when I say.'

Dempsey held his breath as he saw the door open and then through the sights he saw Makepeace. She looked frightened, like a cornered rabbit, as she cautiously eased out of the doorway and then closed the door behind her. There were six steps from the doorway to the pavement, and as she turned towards the street and took the first step down, Dempsey fired.

She crashed back onto the door and then fell heavily down the steps, rolling twice before she hit the pavement. She lay perfectly still, face down, and Dempsey threw the rifle onto the back seat and got out.

'What are you doing?' Davros yelled.

85

'I'm gonna get the sweatshirt, melon-head! You want the police to run a check on it?' and he ran along the pavement and bent over Makepeace. He pulled the jacket from her and then roughly hauled the sweatshirt over her head. Davros pulled up in the car and Dempsey dived into the back.

'Okay, let's go!' he shouted, and the Rolls once again leapt forward as Davros accelerated hard.

'You did well!' he shouted, and the big car swung left at the bottom of the road, but Dempsey said nothing as he felt the fresh sticky blood round the small hole in the chest of the sweatshirt. He looked out at the passing shops as they drove fast through Swiss Cottage, and he wanted to be sick as he felt the blood congealing on his fingers, and somewhere in the distance he heard the urgent braying of an ambulance and he started to shake.

Spikings ran through the rain towards Makepeace and lay panting by her prostrate body. He felt the wet of the ground through his trousers as he knelt on the hard flagstones and he touched her shoulder. She lay, arms outstretched, face down, and her face was covered with her wet blonde hair. The rain began to fall more heavily now, and her back glistened in the street lighting. She was naked from the waist up, and Spikings felt strangely embarrassed.

Seconds later cars seemed to come from all directions and looking up amid the shouting and panic, he saw Morris who was standing over them both.

'Get a blanket, Morris, there's a good lad.'

CHAPTER SEVEN

The front room in No. 4 Hanover Terrace was elegant; decorated and furnished in sympathy with the period and style of the house. The only thing not in keeping with the decor was a large television mounted in the centre of the floor-to-ceiling bookcase. To the right of the bookcase was an ornate marble fireplace and a log fire was burning in the grate.

Merle stood in front of the fire. She still wore black, but she had let her hair down so that it fell easily on her shoulders. She sipped at her Martini and watched the news on the screen with a casual indifference. She heard the front door open and close, and she knew it would be Davros returning with Schwartz. She checked her hair in the mirror above the fireplace, reduced the sound on the television and turned to greet them.

Davros came in the room first.

'Did you get the girl?'

Davros grinned from ear to ear. 'Did we get the girl? Our man Mr Schwartz here took care of her real good – whoever she was – right here,' and he poked a stubby finger at his own heart. 'And then he goes up to the body and tears the sweatshirt off her back, right there in the street. Pretty smart eh?'

Merle smiled at Dempsey. 'You just earned yourself some extra commission, Mr Schwartz.'

Dempsey's eyes narrowed, and he wondered how long he could keep up the act; he was already starting to feel pretty flaky.

'How come?' he asked and tried a grin.

'Each one of those sweatshirts has approximately fifteen hundred pounds of impregnated grade four heroin.'

Dempsey swallowed hard. 'No kidding – that's neat. Real neat.'

'Didn't you know, Mr Schwartz?' Merle looked surprised. 'I thought your people in New York had been told – the cost of the extraction comes out of your end of the deal.'

'We kind'a figured that that was some kind of slush money – to grease a few palms.'

Dempsey was feeling his back to the wall and he knew that if he wasn't careful he'd make another mistake that might prove fatal.

'Good heavens no – it's a very complicated process, perfected by one of our people who used to work in the research department of one of the big textile companies. The powder is mixed with a special solution that puts it in suspension and then it's either sprayed or dipped and then dried onto the fabric.' She paused. 'I'm sorry – would you care for a drink, you look as though you could use one.'

Dempsey nodded at the first sensible suggestion of the day. 'Have you gotta bourbon? I could use a bourbon.'

She nodded to Davros. 'We have most things here, Mr Schwartz – all you have to do is ask.' There was innuendo in the remark that Dempsey chose to ignore. His mind was in a whirl and then, as Davros handed him the drink, Dempsey saw the face of Spikings on the TV screen. The other two ignored the picture and Dempsey took a slug of bourbon and tried to lipread. Spikings was being interviewed by a group of reporters as he was getting into his car.

The reporters jostled, thrusting their tape-recorders and microphones forward, like fat ladies on the first day of the January sales. Morris was doing his best at holding them back, but they pressed forward, eager and hungry for just a hint from Chief Superintendent Spikings.

'Get back now,' Morris shouted into the battery of

reporters, and tried to open the rear door of the car. 'There'll be an official statement made later through the appropriate channels.' He pushed the reporters back and slipped his governor into the car like a ball in a loose scrum.

Spikings touched the driver on the shoulder. 'Hang on,' he said, and lowered the window.

The ladies at the sale thrust their microphones into the open window and someone shouted, 'Was it one of your officers shot here this evening, Superintendent?'

And another shouted, 'Was it a policewoman, sir, who was shot?'

Spikings looked up at the man and spoke in a formal, almost solemn voice. 'There will be an announcement later this evening. A police officer has been involved in a shooting, but before any details can be released, the next of kin have to be informed. That's all I have to say at this moment in time. Thank you.' And he tapped the driver on the shoulder again and raised the window of the car.

'Get me outta here, Harris.'

The car moved away, parting the reporters like the Red Sea, and disappeared into the night.

'Eaton Place, Harris, opposite the St John Ambulance Brigade HQ – and quick!'

The bourbon had gone in Dempsey's glass as he watched the mute performance and he'd been unaware that one of the Koreans had come silently into the room, and was standing obediently behind him at the door. Merle had been talking to Davros but Dempsey had no idea what had been talked about. He just stared at the screen and watched his new boss drive away into the night.

'Ah! Charlie wants to know what we want to eat.' Merle looked over Dempsey's shoulder at the Korean. Dempsey turned in surprise and looked at the Korean called Charlie. The man stood still, and then began to gesticulate with his hands, in sign-language. Merle watched and then turned to Dempsey.

'He's a deaf mute – like his brother. He says that the man on the TV was a policeman, and that a woman cop had been killed – looks like you hit the headlines already.'

Davros waved the man away, and switched off the weather forecast. 'This is more serious – how come she was at the warehouse wearing one of those shirts – how come she got it from that spade – and who was he?'

Merle poured herself another Martini.

'Don't worry, Davros – there's no time for the police to interfere. We will do the deal as soon as Mister Schwartz can arrange it.'

She turned to Dempsey. 'You have the telephone number of the other party, Mister Schwartz?'

Dempsey nodded. 'I was gonna ring them tomorrow.'

'Tomorrow may be cutting it a bit fine – ring them tonight if you will, and arrange for the exchange to take place tomorrow.'

'Tomorrow is Sunday!' Davros interjected.

'Since when has religion had anything to do with business? Try to fix it for tomorrow, Mr Schwartz; if they want the stuff they'll find the money – and I'm sure that Mr Schwartz wants to get back to New York as fast as possible – say, on Monday?' She looked at Dempsey and smiled. 'It is always a problem with following an illegal vocation – always everything is done in a rush. Don't you agree, Mister Schwartz?'

Once again there was innuendo, but this time Dempsey responded, 'I never do anything in a rush – if it's worth doing, that is.'

She averted her gaze and stared into the fire and Dempsey knew that he could have her any time he wanted, and bizarre as it felt to him, he wanted her.

'What about this?' Davros held up the blood-stained

sweatshirt and Dempsey's ardour cooled instantly, but his curiosity still lingered.

He said, 'Maybe I can take it to the processer. I'd like to see the system – maybe we could set up a facility in the States. Might make the deal a whole lot smoother.'

Merle took the sweatshirt from Davros and came to stand close to Dempsey. She had her back to the big Greek and she held the shirt between them, offering it to him.

'Take it,' she said. 'Davros will give you the address, but come back soon – we'll have dinner waiting.'

Dempsey looked down at the sweatshirt and as he took it he saw her finger push through the bullet-hole and then disappear quickly, leaving little to the imagination. He took it and forced a grin and for the first time noticed her perfume. It had a thick, heady floral smell, very animal. It was Bal à Versailles and freshly applied.

'I'll rush right back, ma'am.'

'You do that,' she said, without taking her eyes from him, and she momentarily held on to the shirt, as if teasing.

Spikings's car slid to a halt outside the London house of Lord Winfield, and Spikings got out.

He leant inside the car and spoke softly to the driver. 'Harris, you can go back to the bosom of your family, I'll get a cab home.'

Harris looked concernedly at his governor. 'It's all right, boss – I'll wait.'

But Spikings shook his head. 'No, it's okay, lad, this may take some time. See you tomorrow. G'night.' And he slammed the car door and banged on the roof twice with the palm of his hand. The car drove away and he watched it go for a second. Then he turned to the black front door of Lord Winfield's house and rang the bell. There was no immediate reply, and he stood back on the pavement and looked up. On the first floor he saw a light and he returned to the door and rang the bell again. After a polite elapse of time he rang for a third time and from inside the house he heard footsteps. The hall light went on, and the door opened.

Spikings looked at the old man and said respectfully, 'Is Lord Winfield at home?'

The old man nodded his head impatiently. 'That's me – I'm Lord Winfield,' and he jerked a thumb in the direction of the hall. 'By the time my man has negotiated the stairs from the kitchen, all but the most determined callers have buggered off – who are you?'

'I'm Chief Superintendent Spikings, sir, your daughter's boss. I wonder if I might have a word, sir?'

'Spikings! Didn't recognize you in the dark. Come in me dear chap, come in,' and he ushered Spikings into his house and closed the door.

'Here, let me take yer coat. Blake! Where the devil are you, you old goat. You're supposed to answer the door, not me. Good God, where is the man?'

Blake appeared from below looking much the worse for the climb.

'I'm sorry, sir, it's the damp, sir, makes me almost seize up. Here, sir,' and he brushed the rain from the shoulders of the coat. 'Nasty night to be out, sir.'

Spikings nodded and grunted a reply.

'Stop fussing, you bloody old cripple. Now, Commander—' and he turned to Spikings – 'come in and have a drink. What's your poison?'

'Chief Superintendent, sir,' Spikings corrected, but the older man hadn't heard. The mistake was picked up by Blake.

'My Lord's a bit deaf of late, sir, best to ignore it,' and then louder, 'Shall I postpone dinner, sir?'

Lord Winfield turned at the foot of the stairs. 'What?'

'I said, shall I postpone dinner, sir?'

'Won't it stretch to two?'

'Yes, sir.'

'Well stretch it – you've not eaten, Commander?'

Spikings moved from foot to foot. 'No sir.'

'Right, that settles it. Blake, get a bottle of the

Montrachet, there's a good fellow,' and he turned to climb the stairs and then stopped. 'We haven't drunk it all, have we, Blake – the Montrachet?'

Blake shook his head. 'No, sir – we still have a bottle left, sir.'

'Good God – only one bottle. Have we drunk the rest?'

Blake nodded. 'I'm afraid we have, sir,' but he didn't really include himself.

'Very well,' and he winked at Spikings. 'Can't really leave just one – they don't keep so well on their own. Crack it open, Blake – we'll be upstairs. C'mon Commander.' Spikings contemplated the beginnings of what would have been a very weak protest, and then followed Lord Winfield up the stairs obediently.

They sat at opposite ends of the dining room and Spikings knew that what he had to say to Lord Winfield was going to be difficult.

'Blake always does for two,' he said, looking out of the window and across the street. 'Thinks I don't know, says he makes do with a sandwich. Hmph! Thinks I'm soft in the head more like,' and he got up, walked to the door and shouted impatiently, 'Blake, Blake! Where is the bloody man?'

Spikings moved uncomfortably in his chair. 'Lord Winfield . . .' but Blake came through the door as he spoke and any further conversation on the part of Spikings would have been wasted breath.

'I brought the wine, sir – I'll be up directly with the supper. I thought that we ought to let it breathe a bit . . .'

'Breathe man! Since when has wine ever been around long enough in this house to breathe? Go and get the grub man and stop pissing about. Here, give me that, you're waving the bloody thing round like the winner of the Monte Carlo Grand Prix. This stuff's been lying, minding its own business, for yonks and along you come and treat it like a bottle of dandelion and burdock,' and he took the dusty bottle from Blake and waved him away.

'Harriet's idea is that I should look after Blake, and sometimes I think she's right. Now then, let's crack this open; I think you'll like it.'

He opened a drawer, took out a corkscrew and carefully began to remove the cork. 'Now then, what is it you've come to see me about? Is she in hot water? In the club, or what? Hello, I think this cork's going to be a bit naughty. Here, you have a go.'

The lights on the fifth floor of Grosvenor Place were subdued and Lei Shan sat at her desk and watched the information changing on the grey screen. Her birdlike fingers pecked at the keyboard and such was her concentration, that she almost ignored the telephone, its shrill tone sounding louder at night than during the day. She flicked the 'hold' button on the keyboard and picked up the telephone but her mind was still totally involved in the screenful of green figures.

'Hello,' she said, her almond shaped eyes slightly narrowed as she read the flickering figures, but when she heard the American voice at the other end of the telephone, her eyes widened and she sat back from her work. 'I was expecting a call from you on Monday. There is no problem, I trust?' and she found great difficulty in stifling instant hatred as she heard the voice of her mother's murderer.

'No – no problem at all.' The voice sounded clean and strong and she wished for a moment that it had not sounded so honest. 'It's just that we have a minor problem at our end and I'd like to bring the deal forward; it would help us considerably.'

'How much would helping you considerably mean – in terms of an adjustment to the final figure?' Lei Shan's powers of bargaining had not deserted her totally, even though revenge consumed her mind.

94

'I guess we could do a deal, no harm in that. What d'you say to a reduction of fifty grand?'

She was silent for a moment, and then she asked, '. . . and when?'

'Tomorrow.'

'Tomorrow? I cannot get hold of two million dollars by tomorrow – it is impossible.'

'Less fifty grand – that's a helluva discount baby.'

'Ring me back in two hours time – I shall have to see what I can do. Will you ring?'

'Sure,' and the phone went dead. She sat very still for fully a minute, and then pressed a buzzer on the desk. The money was no problem, she already had it, but the other arrangement would take some time to put into operation. The final extermination of Schwartz.

Dempsey put the phone down. 'Two million! That's a lotta dope. That's a lotta kids dead,' and he thanked the barman for the use of the phone and ordered another drink. Somehow he had to get to Spikings before he got back to Lei Shan, and he had to find out about Makepeace.

'Will that be all, sir?' Blake stood by the side of Lord Winfield, patiently waiting to be dismissed.

'Yes, yes Blake, you may go. We'll have coffee downstairs. Thank you,' and he waved his old batman away. Blake closed the door behind him and shuffled off downstairs shaking his head. He hoped nothing was wrong with Miss Harriet and wondered why Chief Superintendent Spikings should call on his Lordship in the evening, unannounced.

Spikings lifted the glass of Montrachet, inspected the colour and took a swig. 'Bloody good drop of stuff, sir,' he said and took another.

'Not bad – couldn't buy it now for love nor money. I've had this for years, rather sad in a way to be drinking the last bottle. Still, every good thing must come to an end I suppose. Cheers,' and he raised his glass and sniffed the bouquet of the wine before sipping a small amount. 'God, that's good! Now, Commander – I presume you've come to see me about my daughter. Well, spit it out man – what's the trouble?'

CHAPTER EIGHT

Dempsey left the bar in the Holiday Inn at Swiss Cottage, and got a cab to the address that Davros had given him, just off the Kilburn High Road. It was a barber's shop with a striped pole outside, and he rang the bell of the side door and after a short pause he heard a voice over an entryphone system.

'Who's that?'

'The name's Schwartz – I'm delivering one more shirt for processing.'

There was another brief pause and then the voice said, 'Where have you come from, Mister Schwartz?'

'From Merle and Davros.' The buzzer sounded and the shabby door swung open. He descended the dimly lit stairs to a basement room that smelt of neat heroin. A man stood at the bottom of the stairs and Dempsey could tell he was wearing a piece.

'I brought the last garment – it got kinda diverted and I had to go retrieve it.'

The man took the shirt and held it up. He inspected the hole in the shirt and raised an eyebrow. 'Is this blood?'

'It sure ain't ketchup.'

'I'll have to cut out the stained area, otherwise we could well have an adverse reaction. The last batch is going to the processor in the next hour – do you wish to wait?

'Nope – I've got to get on back – I'll let myself out,' and he turned on his heel and walked back up the stairs to the front door. Outside, the air smelt sweet and fresh in comparison with the basement.

'Another half hour down there and I'd have been as high as the Empire State,' he said aloud and walked over the road to a phone box that, to his surprise, had not received a full frontal lobotomy. He rang through to S.I.10 and spoke to the duty officer. He gave him the details of the processing plant, asked for Spikings's home address, and got another cab. Time was running out. He had to try and get to Spikings and then get back to Merle.

Spikings had picked up his own car from the Chelsea nick and was driving home. He drove slowly and had the volume on his radio turned high. The last few bars of Mozart's Piano No. 21 in C Major was playing and Spikings was more with the music than the traffic. The piece ended and as the applause from the audience rose, he turned down the volume and smiled as he turned to his passenger.

'Magic,' he said.

His passenger returned his smile and said, 'I didn't know you were a Mozart fan.'

'That, I'll have you know, is the theme music from Elvira Madigan.'

'By Mozart.'

Spikings looked back at the traffic. 'I suppose you're a bloody classics buff, along with everything else, eh, 'arry?'

She laughed out loud and tossed her blonde hair back out of her eyes. 'Not really – but I'd put a fiver on it,' and she turned up the volume on the radio just in time to win her bet.

'Told you so.'

The announcer on the radio continued, 'The time is ten o'clock. Here is the news. This evening in London, an officer of the plain-clothes division of the Metropolitan police was shot dead. So far there are no details of the incident, but a full statement is expected soon. The identity of the officer is being withheld until the next of kin have been informed. In the Lebanon today . . .'

Spikings turned the radio off and looked across again at his passenger.

98

'Incidentally,' she said, 'how did Daddy take the news of my death?'

Spikings smiled again. 'With a Havana in one hand . . .'

'. . . and a Scotch in the other,' she completed.

'Having just forced down some cold salmon, new potatoes and a bottle of Chassagne-Montrachet, slightly chilled.'

'It's good to know that austerity is still biting hard in Eaton Place,' she said sarcastically. 'So while I was being rather unceremoniously bundled out the back of Hammersmith morgue, you were having a gay old time with father and swilling down a bottle of the family's best Montrachet.'

Spikings rubbed his chin to conceal the smirk on his face. 'The last bottle actually.'

'Bloody hell, has the old goat ripped his way through the lot! We brought it from the cellars of the British Embassy in Rome when my father gave up the Diplomatic Service. It was about the only sensible thing he ever did – and now it's gone.'

'Rome? I didn't know you were in Rome, 'arry. That must account for why you and Dempsey hit it off so well. His mother was from Rome.'

'Presumably a tart from the Via Veneto who got put up the club by his half-Irish father – God, what a combination.'

Spikings laughed. 'No – I suppose he's about as faraway from your sort as could be. But for a mongrel he thinks pretty quick on his feet. That wheeze of his this evening got him out of a bloody tight jam and no mistake.'

'I just couldn't believe what I was seeing when I wandered into that bloody warehouse – talk about rotten luck or coincidence or whatever. Poor old Dempsey must have been wetting himself.' She paused, reflecting on the activity of the day. 'Any news on the other two, Ziggy's mates?'

Spikings shook his head. 'No – not a bloody sausage.

But I'm sure that Dempsey will have found out by now. I don't reckon much for their chances. Ziggy didn't see the afternoon through, and that was in broad bloody daylight.'

'Poor Ziggy.' Makepeace sighed and wondered if her dear dead mother would ever forgive her for choosing such an extraordinary career.

The car turned down a ramp that led into an underground car park, and Spikings seemed to relax a little.

'Well – here we are. It's not exactly the Ritz, but it's home.'

'Do you live alone, sir?'

Spikings chortled. 'It may appear to the outside world, 'arry, that I'm the centrefold of Playgirl, but no, there is the redoubtable Mrs Spikings to keep me out of trouble.'

Makepeace looked worried. 'She won't mind – my staying I mean. I could go back to the flat – or to Daddy's if it would be better.'

He shook his head. 'No, no – I'm always pitching up with a bit of fluff – hang about, I think we've got company.'

Spikings glanced to his left. 'Over there, did you see?'

Makepeace nodded. 'Don't stop, just slow down and park,' and before Spikings had slowed the vehicle Makepeace opened the passenger door and rolled out onto the concrete floor.

The lights were dim, and as she crouched behind the line of parked cars she saw for a second time the movement in the shadows, and she heard the scrape of a foot. Her breathing was coming fast now and she moved down the back wall, hugging whatever cover she could find. Spikings eased the car into his parking bay and stopped, and as he applied the handbrake he took the .38 Webley from the glove compartment and switched off.

Makepeace heard the handbrake being applied, and

100

saw the dark figure moving closer to Spikings' car. She
was about twenty yards away from the car and behind
a thick concrete pillar, when she heard the car door
open and saw the bulky figure of her boss heave
himself out of the front seat. The figure closed in on
Spikings and so did she. Spikings paused for a moment
and then slammed his door shut, and as he did so
Makepeace made her final move towards the crouching
figure that was between her and Spikings.

'Don't move, stand perfectly still. I am police and I
am armed.' Her voice was steady and ice-cold. There
was a brief pause and Spikings turned, holding his
revolver in both hands, and the man stood up.

'I bet a month's pay, Makepeace, you've still got the
safety catch applied.'

'Dempsey, what the hell are you doing here?' and
she leant heavily on the car. 'I nearly blew your damned
head off!'

'Well – I figured I had to see you, sir, and fill in a few
details,' and he looked at Makepeace, 'and make sure
old Makepeace here was okay. I was kinda worried
with the TV and all.'

'Fooled you, did we?' she said and grinned at him.

'It was the blood that threw me a bit.'

'Best Angus steak, fresh from my fridge.'

'No kidding?'

Spikings interrupted them. 'When you two have
quite finished, perhaps we can draw this touching
little reunion to a close. I think you'd better get back,
Dempsey. We'll arrange to contact you on Monday.'

'It'll all be over by Monday – the whole thing's
opened wide, the meet's tomorrow.'

'Why the panic?' asked Spikings, and Dempsey
jerked a thumb in the direction of Makepeace.

'There'd be no panic if she hadn't come swaggering
into that warehouse. How come you pitch up there
anyway? I was just getting my feet under the table; I
got something going with the chick in black and then

– wham! In strolls Makepeace here, wearing one of their goddam sweatshirts.'

'I didn't know you were there – I didn't know it was one of their bloody little sweatshirts – and just for the record, I don't sweat.'

'You know why I pulled it off you outside your apartment? It's impregnated with grade four heroin, that's why.'

'What!' Spikings and Makepeace chorused and then Spikings snapped his fingers.

'That's the stuff that came in on that bloody container truck, boxed videos and garments. No wonder they couldn't find anything when they pulled it apart.'

'They put the stuff in a special solution that puts it in suspension, and then they just spray it onto the fabric. Then the whole process gets reversed.'

'Where, here?'

'Yup, right here in a place off Kilburn High Road. I gave the address to your duty officer earlier – but right now we got a big problem. I've gotta fix the exchange for tomorrow. It's two million bucks' worth of stuff, so it's pretty big. But I gotta get back to this Lei Shan broad before eleven tonight to tell her where. I thought you guys could maybe suggest somewhere.'

Spikings looked at Makepeace and then at his watch. 'What time have you to get back to the house at Hanover Terrace?'

Dempsey shrugged. 'I dunno. I guess it don't matter too much, but I haven't got a key.'

Makepeace raised an eyebrow. 'I'm sure that the black widow will wait up for you.'

'That's what I'm afraid of.'

'After your body, is she, Dempsey? Well, just remember – don't get involved with the customers, it makes for complications later.'

Dempsey grinned. 'Don't worry, sir, my honour will remain intact – even if she doesn't. I don't think she's my type anyway.'

102

'She looked a bit high-class, I must say,' Makepeace responded and winked at Spikings.

'I can handle high-class broads, Sergeant, they've never phased me in the past. But,' and he became very serious, 'she's very heavy – I mean, *very* heavy. The two guys on the bust last night . . .'

Makepeace also became serious. 'What happened to them?'

'I ain't got the precise details, but I don't reckon we stand much chance of finding their bodies. I think Tweedle-dum and Tweedle-dee did a pretty good disposal job, from what I heard – but so far they haven't said much. That broad Merle though, she is something else again,' he looked at Spikings, 'so don't worry on my account, I ain't gonna tangle with that chick.'

'And who's this Lei Shan woman?' Spikings asked. 'Where does she fit in?'

Dempsey shrugged. 'I guess she's the front lady for the money; she's a big wheel in a West End merchant banking operation that's into North Sea oil. Chinese, ex-Laos, ex-Thailand. I guess she's come all the way down the poppy trail – but she's put the money together in London. She's the link-person as far as the mob in New York are concerned. What we gotta do is to make sure we get all these cats under one tin roof tomorrow so we can do a bit of permanent dental surgery – you know, we're the guys fighting urban decay an' all – let's pull some of the bastards out by the roots, you know what I mean?'

Makepeace smiled. 'I have a pretty shrewd idea, but I don't think that even our beloved Prime Minister would go along with total extraction where perhaps just filling a cavity would suffice, but I do get your point.' And she applied the safety catch to her revolver so that Dempsey could see that the action was deliberate, and returned it to the holster.

'Where were you intending to call the Chinese woman from?' Spikings asked.

'From a box I guess.'

'If we drop you off near the Hanover Terrace house you could call her from there, couldn't you?'

'I guess.'

'Well – let's go – we don't want to keep your paramour waiting, do we?' and he opened the rear door of his car and Dempsey got in. Spikings looked at Makepeace and she took the hint and got into the back next to Dempsey.

The car drove out of the car park and Dempsey looked at Makepeace in a very personal way and touched her hand.

'I was kinda worried about you, what with the TV back-up an' all. Thought for a moment I might have blown you away.'

She fought the temptation to grab his hand, particularly as they were being driven by their boss, so she patted the back of it instead.

'I thought we all did rather well, until you decided to come and yank that T-shirt off my back.' She paused. 'If I'd known that was part of the plan, I'd have worn a liberty bodice.'

Dempsey asked in genuine ignorance, 'What the hell's a liberty bodice?'

'It's a little English number that prevents them from being taken – liberties that is.'

'There's an old warehouse opposite Butler's Wharf on the north side of the river next to St Katharine's Dock.' Spikings looked in the rear-view mirror and saw that Dempsey and Makepeace were looking at each other in an odd way. '. . . and you can stop any jiggery-pokery in the back of my car, you two.'

'Butler's Wharf, sir?'

'Opposite Butler's Wharf, Makepeace, on the north side. It might be a good place for a meet tomorrow. The city's quiet on Sunday, and Tower Hamlets' river side is even quieter. We could have all our lads in position down there by first light, and if there was a punch-up and they cut and ran, then we'd not get snarled up in a lot of traffic.'

'What's the name of the warehouse?' Dempsey asked, taking his hand away from Makepeace's.

'Dunno – I'll get one of the boys to find out,' and he picked up the radio handset and called into S.1.10.

Dempsey rang the bell of No. 4 Hanover Terrace and was let into the house by Davros. The man smelt of garlic and sweat and he'd been drinking. He steadied himself on the doorway before he went back into the drawing room and Dempsey could feel an obvious hostility from the big Greek.

Merle had changed and was curled up on the sofa in front of the fire. She was wearing a brilliant red silk cheong-sam and when Dempsey came into the room, she stood up. As she turned to face him he noticed too that the regulation slit up one side of her dress seemed to go far above and beyond what was usual. Davros went to pour himself another drink without looking at either Dempsey or Merle.

'Davros gotta problem?' Dempsey asked, jerking his head in the direction of the big man.

'He's got a bad attack of jealousy, I think.' She shrugged. 'Don't let it concern you – he's quite harmless when I'm around. I'll send him to bed shortly. I've kept supper for us – you've been a long time?'

Dempsey grinned. 'I had a few details to sort out, and I made a check on the place we meet tomorrow.'

'Is it fixed?'

'I gotta phone – may I?' and he moved across the room to the telephone by the window. She nodded and sat down again on the sofa. The dress fell away as she sat, and Dempsey's eyes popped as she crossed her legs, revealing almond-coloured skin up to and beyond her thigh. There were no prizes for guessing she wore nothing beneath the cheong-sam and Dempsey kept looking as he dialled the number. Merle smiled, leaving no doubt in Dempsey's mind that the lady had only one thing on her mind, and it wasn't Davros. She clasped her hands around her knee and leant back a little, pulling her knee towards her body, revealing the inner thigh of her left leg. She smiled more positively at Dempsey as he waited for his call to connect. He heard the phone ring twice and then the voice of Lei Shan.

'Hello?'

'Lei Shan – it's Schwartz. Have we a deal?'

Merle raised one eyebrow in anticipation.

'We have a deal, Mr Schwartz.'

Dempsey nodded at Merle. 'Ten o'clock tomorrow,' he said and Merle looked at her watch.

'Where?'

'At Drew's Wharf. On the north bank of the river, just east of Tower Bridge.'

Dempsey listened to a brief silence and then Lei Shan spoke.

'That will be acceptable. The money is in mixed denominations, all used and non-sequential, less fifty thousand. It will be in two cases. Don't be late, Mister Schwartz, I shall be waiting for you,' and she hung up. Dempsey replaced the telephone and smiled at Merle.

'We have a deal.'

'We certainly do,' she said and Dempsey knew she didn't mean the next morning.

'Mind if I fix myself a drink?' He walked over to her and put his hand on her knee. 'By the way – I don't think that man mountain over there should get any more juiced-up tonight. Tomorrow may not be a picnic.'

'Why d'you say that?'

'Because things are never as straightforward as they seem. There's always a dozen reasons why something simple like this can foul up, and if he's slowed up with booze, then he ain't the guy to be on my side. You know what I mean?'

'Davros,' her voice had an edge to it that made him turn towards them both.

'Yes?'

106

'Don't drink any more, Davros – Mr Schwartz and I don't think that it's prudent. Okay?'

Davros finished the tumblerful of whisky in one and gave Dempsey a look that didn't need any translation.

'The stuff will be ready to pick up from Kilburn by six in the morning – don't foul up, Davros, or you're gonna be eating hospital food for a long time. You got the message, fat man?' Davros blinked at Dempsey and looked at Merle.

'He's right,' she said simply, and there was an awkward moment as Davros swayed, hesitated and then turned clumsily and slowly left the room.

Merle breathed a sigh of relief. 'I thought for one horrible moment he was going to turn ugly.'

'I thought he already was ugly,' and Dempsey walked over to where Davros had been drinking.

'Can I fix you something?' he asked casually.

'No more for me – besides, I don't need it.'

Dempsey looked at her and for a moment wished that it was another time and another place. He poured himself a stiff bourbon and raised his glass. 'To tomorrow eh?' and he sipped the bourbon.

'What's wrong with tonight? It's okay you know – I've done my homework.'

Dempsey didn't know what she meant and so grinned and shrugged as if he understood.

'The boys on 43rd Street were very forthcoming about some of your little, how shall we say, vices,' and she stroked her thigh as she spoke. 'So, like I said – it's all right.'

She stood up, pushed the creases from her dress and walked towards Dempsey. He smelt her perfume again, but this time it was more musky somehow. She stopped when she was very close and put her arms around his neck. Dempsey stood still and there was a moment of silence.

'I'll get supper now,' she said and lifted her face to his, gently brushing her lips across his mouth and tasting the bourbon. Dempsey put the glass down and pulled her to him and she tasted more bourbon, but this time with her tongue. He ran his left hand down her side and slipped it between the high cut slit of the cheong-sam. He felt her stiffen and the bare cheek of her backside contracted and was hard and taut.

'I'll get dinner,' she said, and pulled away from him. 'I like my men on a full stomach,' and she swayed gracefully out of the room leaving Dempsey half-aroused and strangely uncomfortable, and he thought of Makepeace in the back of Spikings's car, and earlier when he so narrowly missed her under the eagle eye of Davros.

He sat down heavily and picked up his drink. There was something about Merle that he found deeply disturbing; something about her that he found profoundly unnerving, something sinister. He finished his drink and went through into the dining room.

The table was Georgian, D-ended and very elegantly laid with two place settings at either end. Merle pressed a bell, and Dempsey heard the distant ring in another part of the house. There was another fire laid and burning in a similar marble setting and the room was dark, lit only by four small wall-lights that were dimmed, and the fire. Dempsey sat at one end of the table and Merle came to him and stood behind him. She placed her hands on his shoulders and they gazed in silence at the flickering wood fire.

Dempsey looked up at Merle and said, 'Cosy huh?' She smiled and ran a finger up the nape of his neck, and once again he felt the sinister overtone of her silence. There was a soft knock on the door and without waiting for a response, the door opened and the two Koreans came in. One wheeled a Hostess trolley and the other carried a tray of drinks. Without a word they prepared and served the meal, dispensed the wine and silently left the room. Merle had remained standing behind Dempsey while this had gone on, and only after they had left did she move, and as she did so she dug her fingernails into the back of Dempsey's neck, as if in anticipation of what was to follow.

Dempsey winced slightly, reached for one of the hot blinis that were piled high on a plate in front of him, and watched Merle as she moved gracefully to the other end of the table and sat facing him. She too took one of the yeast pancakes made from buckwheat flour, lifted the lid from a silver tureen that had been set before her and spooned the Bulgar caviar onto the blini. Dempsey did likewise with a similar tureen and guessed that there must have been about half a pound of pressed caviar surrounded by crushed ice in each tureen. The lady don't do things by half, he thought, as he figured that good caviar would retail at about $300 a pound.

Merle lifted her tall glass and held it towards Dempsey. 'To a morning of mutual satisfaction.'

Dempsey didn't quite know what she meant, but he guessed it had sexual overtones and he wondered what in hell she'd meant by his 'vices according to the boys on 43rd Street'. He lifted his glass, 'I'll drink to that,' and he blinked as he felt the first cold wash of vodka hit the back of his throat, like a surgical mouthwash. 'Jesus!'

She smiled at him in a superior, but approving way, like a stud owner would look at a newly acquired stallion.

'It's the only thing to drink with caviar, don't you think so?'

'It sure as hell beats the ass off a warm beer. Cheers!' and he spooned more caviar, washed it down with the Russian gargle, and felt his eyes begin to water.

Merle rang again when the caviar was finished and the Koreans appeared, cleared away the debris, and served them each with a large rare T-bone steak, large even by American standards. Dempsey looked at the bottle of wine offered for his approval by one of the Koreans.

'It's a '66 Hermitage, referred to by Johnson as the

"manliest" of wines. Dark, powerful and profound. I think you'll like it,' and she nodded to the Korean to open the bottle. He did so and offered some to Dempsey to taste.

Dempsey sipped the wine and nodded his approval. 'Tastes pretty manly to me. Who the hell's this Johnson anyhow – some kinda wine faggot?'

Merle cut into her steak and watched the blood run on her plate. The rare meat was good, and she ate delicately, but quickly.

'Tell me what you have in mind for tomorrow – what arrangements have you made?' and she continued to eat her steak and pick at the side salad.

'Well, this is the way of it. Davros collects the stuff in the morning and we all get to Drew's Wharf at about a quarter after ten.'

Merle's fork stopped for a second before she ate the next mouthful of meat. 'I thought you said ten o'clock on the phone.'

'We get there late so they're edgy – believe me, I know what I'm doing.' He pointed at her with his knife as he spoke. 'Don't forget – we get two million bucks in cash and the stuff. Now, its street value may be worth, I dunno,' he shrugged, 'twice that amount, so all together we got six million bucks sitting all together. Now that's a lotta dough, enough to buy an army of hoodlums to blast in and take the lot. So we gotta be careful. We know this Lei Shan dame – and she's okay. If she fucks up on this one it'll be her last bit of business, so I don't have too many worries on that score, but you can never be sure. Sometimes it's the number ones and number twos who get greedy. Always watch the back-up man. He's liable to fill you full of lead and make a quick buck. You know what I mean?' Dempsey pushed his plate away from him and sat back in his chair, wondering if he sounded like New York Mafia.

She nodded, 'I guess I trust you,' she said.

'I guess you have to but if this deal goes through

110

without any problems then we can do it all over again. Maybe on a regular basis.'

'I'd like that, Mr Schwartz.'

At the back of the house was a small paved courtyard, and large terracotta tubs for plants were spaced regularly around its edge. The tubs were full of black earth and peat and all the vegetation of the summer had died away and was brown and limp. On the three sides of the courtyard there was a six foot brick wall with two foot of wooden trellis above that, and it was the wooden trellis that snapped like a pistol shot in the night air that momentarily stopped the heart of Makepeace as she hitched her leg over it, and then dropped down heavily into the garden.

'Shit!' she swore under her breath, and crouched very still behind one of the large tubs and waited. She was breathing hard and as she waited she could feel the cold seeping through the thin soles of her boots, and then she caught her breath again as the outside light at the back door went on. She heard a key turn in the lock, and then another shaft of yellow light stabbing into the courtyard and one of the Koreans appeared in the doorway. He stood for a while and then took out a reefer and lit it, inhaling deeply and looking up at the night sky. Makepeace watched him as he smoked and forced herself as hard as she could against the old yellow brickwork of the wall.

He leant on the doorway as the lazy smoke from the reefer washed over him and he relaxed into a state of semi-trance. She lay still, not daring to move and then to her horror he began to walk into the courtyard, towards the terracotta tub she hid behind. She held her breath and very slowly moved her head so that she could see his approach more clearly. There was no way of escape and although she was armed, the thought of a gun-shot in that garden at night, with Dempsey inside the house, would be her second big mistake of the day. She moved her right hand fractionally and felt

111

a single loose brick tucked behind the terracotta tub. It felt cold and rough, and the edges were sharp and new.

The Korean was about ten feet from the tub she was crouched behind, and she reckoned that if she was very quick she could probably jump him. One good blow to the head with her sharp new brick, and with the element of surprise on her side, One-Hung-Low would be out cold, allowing Makepeace time to shin back over the wall and start again. She moved her legs up towards her and eased into a semi-crouch, like a cat ready to spring.

The man stopped at the next tub along the wall and for a moment Makepeace froze. He looked up again at the sky, placed the reefer firmly between his lips, unzipped his trousers and urinated into the tub. Makepeace stared at the bizarre sight, and in the cold refined silence of a London January evening she watched the all-yellow rainbow, caught in the light from the kitchen, as it cascaded into the dead winter weeds, like the sound of beer running from the tap of a barrel onto a large empty cellar floor. It sounded as loud and as foreign as the snap of the broken lattice-work.

He stood there with his eyes closed and a smile on his face, breathing in the smoke from the reefer and, quite clearly, experiencing something close to orgasm. Makepeace began to move; now was probably the best time to administer the 'coup de brick' and, as she pulled slowly on the rim of the tub to adjust her balance, he stopped as suddenly as he had started, and without even having the grace to shake off the drops, he stuffed it back into his trousers as quick as a shit-house rat. He stood still and Makepeace froze, feeling her fingers losing purchase on the thick terracotta rim of the tub, and then, still with his eyes closed, he turned on his heel and went back into the house. The door closed quietly and the lights went out and Makepeace released her grip on the brick, let go of the tub and sank back on her haunches against the wall. She let her breath go in one long uncontrolled blow and suddenly was aware that despite the coldness of the night, she was sweating profusely.

CHAPTER NINE

Dempsey looked over the edge of his coffee cup, aware only of the inevitable advance from Merle and unsure of his own defence mechanism. There was something fascinating about her, something animal in her physical make-up that drew men to her like a magnet, like cowboys to a mustang at a rodeo. Ready and eager to ride, but knowing that sooner or later they'd be bucked clean off, and then trampled on, unless they could find cover.

And yet – he looked into her eyes beyond that superficial beauty, and there was something about her that put the fear of Christ into Dempsey – something unhealthy, almost evil. She smiled at him, slowly and deliberately put her coffee cup down, and stood up.

'Well – shall we go up? It's very late,' and she walked to the door, opened it and waited for Dempsey to follow suit. He hesitated briefly and as he stood and felt the effect of the drink he knew that now was not the right time, not the right place, and most certainly Merle was not the right woman.

'We've got an important day tomorrow, I think maybe I'll take a rain check on anything else tonight, Merle. If you don't mind.' He walked towards her and he could smell the heady perfume, and he felt his resolve weakening rapidly. 'Why don't we save it till later – when the heat's off some.'

'I'm better when the heat's on – if you follow my meaning,' and she ran her fingers down the side of his face and pouted as if mildly disappointed. 'But, as you will,' and she swept from the room and began to climb the stairs in the hall. One of the Koreans sat impassively at the foot of the stairs staring blankly in front of him like a farm boy at a Latin lesson, seemingly unaware of Merle as she passed him.

Dempsey followed a few paces behind and looked at the Korean. 'If I were you I'd get your head down. Tomorrow I want you at the Wharf real early.' The Korean sat motionless and looked blankly at Dempsey. 'He don't say a whole lot, does he?' Dempsey called up to Merle.

She placed a hand on her hip and laughed. 'He's a deaf mute – so is his brother.'

'You don't say,' Dempsey replied.

'No, *they* don't, but they're very loyal, like dogs.'

Dempsey walked up the first flight of stairs and once again, like a fly, got closer to the spider. She put her arms round his neck. 'You don't know what you're missing.' She was very close to him now and as their eyes met she dropped one of her arms and pressed the palm of her hand to his crutch. He stood very still, and in the half light on the landing, the pupils of her eyes looked as black as the fruit of sloes.

'Whatever it is, I guess it'll keep,' and he kissed her lips lightly. 'Goodnight Merle.'

He almost tripped as he negotiated the next flight of stairs and he could feel those jet-black eyes boring into his back like twin lasers. He crossed to the next landing, opened the door to his bedroom and closed it quickly. A soft voice behind him made him spin fast on the balls of his feet.

'It would have been the end of a beautiful friendship.'

'Makepeace, what the fuck are you doing here?'

'Oh! Just making sure you stay out of trouble.' She walked towards him, took out a handkerchief and wiped the lipstick from his mouth. 'There, that shade doesn't suit you anyway.'

He almost pushed her hand away. 'Makepeace, what the hell are you trying to do to me?' he hissed. 'This morning you blew this thing open like a can of worms,

115

and now you've done it again. Does Spikings know you're here?'

'No.'

'Jesus-H-Christ.'

'Listen – I've got an idea.'

'You've what?'

'To even up the odds, if you see what I mean.'

'Spikings is gonna have your ass lady – how d'you get in here anyway?'

'Up the drainpipe and into a bathroom. The big Greek is crashed out on his bed fully clothed and fast asleep – he looks drunk even though he's asleep.'

'He is,' nodded Dempsey.

'And the two other little charmers are in the kitchen.'

'How long have you been in the house?'

She looked at her watch. 'Oh, almost an hour, I suppose; some of the stuff in here is very classy, mostly stolen I'd imagine.'

Dempsey turned back to the door, opened it a fraction and, satisfied that Merle was no longer lurking outside, closed the door and locked it.

'Now listen, Sergeant, I appreciate your concern about evening up the numbers, but I don't see really how you can help. Davros is leaving at six in the morning to go back to Kilburn to get the stuff, and the little oriental bastards are leaving at about seven to go check out the warehouse at Drew's Wharf.'

'Will Davros be back before the other two leave?'

Dempsey shrugged. 'I dunno – maybe not. Why?'

'So that would mean that for some time, maybe only a short time, you would be alone with Merle.'

Dempsey's eyes narrowed as he looked at Make-peace. 'If you're gonna suggest what I think you're gonna suggest – the answer, Sergeant, is no, positively and irrevocably no.'

At 05.30 the small alarm clock rang on the bedside table, and for some time Davros slept on. Then the big man stirred, but still the deep sleep held the white pudgy eyelids firmly shut. The alarm clock continued its tinkling reveille, and with a monumental effort Davros fought off the drunken bliss of sleep and he awoke and twitched erect, like some giant puppet from Brobdingnag. His hand groped for the small alarm and crushed it into silence as if it were a grape and he swung his legs off the bed and sat up, rubbing his eyelids into life with as much vigour as a doctor would use on a cardiac arrest. Twenty minutes later, having held his head under the shower attachment for at least half that time, he emerged from his room and went down to the kitchen.

He made coffee, black with four teaspoons of sugar, and he broke three eggs into a large cup, added pepper, an indecent amount of Worcestershire sauce, and drank the lot in one gulp. He then belched, washed the eggs down with the coffee and left the house. It was still dark and he paid no attention to the North Thames Gas Board van which was parked up the road, as he got into the Rolls and drove off.

'Hello Charlie six, the Rolls has just left Number 4. Over.'

'Charlie six, move to your next location. Over.'

'Charlie six, Roger out.'

Spikings sat in his office with Morris. They both looked very tired and they were both smoking.

'Well Morris old son – looks like we're off, as they say.'

'Looks that way, guv,' and he got up and took the cold, undrunk mug of tea from his boss's desk. There was a brown ring left clinging to the inside of the mug and the congealed skin left floating on the surface danced as Morris picked it up.

'You wanna fresh one, guv? I think we've got time.'

'Yeah, why not.' He took a bottle of whisky from the double drawer and thrust it at Morris. 'Here, stick some of that in it, there's a good lad.'

Morris took the bottle and disappeared. Spikings sat

117

back and checked his watch, yawned and then rang Ed Zukko in the Hilton in New York.

'Ed Zukko please, room 1193. Thank you.' There was a short pause and then Spikings heard the sleepy voice of Zukko on the line. 'Ed – sorry to wake you up. It's Gordon. Just thought I'd let you know that we're in business.'

'Is Dempsey okay?'

'So far – well, let's say he was still in one piece a few hours ago. Anyway I'll be in touch. Oh by the way, when it's over if everything works out, do you want Schwartz back again?'

'Sure, just put him on the next plane and I'll have him met by a couple of agents at J.F.K. S'long Gordon. Good luck,' and the phone went dead.

Spikings sat back and lit a cigarette. He felt very tired, and he wondered how long it was going to be before his Commander would put him out to grass. Spikings took out a small battery shaver, and still with the cigarette in his mouth, began to shave. He didn't trust his Commander. Spikings didn't trust most people, but somewhere or other he had a feeling in his water that there was a skeleton in the Commander's cupboard – and most people rattled if they were shaken hard enough.

Morris came in with the tea and set it down amongst the papers on the desk. 'Here we are, guv. Hot and laced.'

'Ta Morris – any news of 'arry by the way?'

'No guv – she must have gone to spend the night with 'er old man. There's no answer from 'er flat. Why, you don't want her involved, do you?'

'No. No. She's done enough already, poor cow. I reckon she's got a bit of a soft spot for old Dempsey you know.'

'Do you guv?'

'Yeah – in the same way as Lady Chatterley.'

'You reckon she'd fancy a bit o' rough, do you?'

'Something like that.'

'Shall I ring her father's place?'

'No – I reckon both her old man and his butler need all the sleep they can get. They're both about to peg out any day now.'

Morris grinned at his boss and nodded at the tea. 'Drink up, sir, we'd best be off – the rest of the boys are already at the location now.'

Spikings sipped the hot tea. 'Jesus, Morris, how much bloody Scotch d'you put in here?'

'Most of it, sir – I thought maybe you might need a little something to keep out the cold.'

Spikings grunted and gulped at the tea until it was finished. 'Okay, Morris, let's get at 'em.'

Morris stared at his boss as he left the office, tasted his own tea, winced and put it down. 'The man's an animal,' he whispered to himself and followed Spikings out into the dawn.

At six-twenty the two Koreans left the house in Hanover Terrace and drove off in an anonymous looking Ford Cortina, and out across Regent's Park the first grey hint of dawn silhouetted Lord Snowdon's bird aviary in the centre of London Zoo. Dempsey watched them go and could feel the cold of the morning on the old thin glass of the sash window. Seconds after the Cortina had disappeared from view he saw the London taxi pull out from a line of cars and follow it at a respectable distance. The park was quiet and then he heard the unmistakable roar of a big cat.

'Makepeace,' he whispered, and looked round into the bedroom. Makepeace was fast asleep on the top of the bedclothes, fully clothed including her Gucci boots. He moved over to her and knelt by the side of the bed. Her blonde hair lay softly on the pillow and Dempsey looked intently at her face. She was almost smiling and he observed that she wasn't wearing any make-up at all. He sniffed at her curiously, trying to determine what kind of smell it was that he felt vaguely in his nostrils.

Makepeace opened one eye. 'What are you doing, Dempsey?'

He pulled back quickly, but remained kneeling. 'I was just wondering what you smelt like.' He knew he'd put that badly. 'I mean, what kinda perfume you've got on – and I was going to wake you up anyway.'

'Oh,' she opened both eyes. 'I see. You haven't been kneeling there all night, sniffing at me like a bag of glue, have you?'

'No, no. The Korean twins have just left, and I guess we ought to make our move pretty soon. Makepeace . . .' he touched her shoulder as she sat up on the bed, 'I just heard a goddamn tiger!'

Makepeace grinned at him. 'They run loose in Regent's Park, didn't you know?'

'They what?'

She giggled quietly and took the hand that was offered and pulled herself off the bed. 'It's the zoo, silly,' and she sounded very English. Dempsey looked at her and resisted the temptation to pull her to him, and suddenly he felt that this frail little English rose of a girl was likely to become more than just his partner.

'Peter Pan,' he said. 'I've just resisted the temptation to say something stupid.'

'Listen, every time you feel the temptation, just have a quick sniff – I don't mind at all.' But in her heart she did, and she wondered how long it would be before their diametrically opposed characters became sufficiently compatible to justify consummation.

'Anyway, I'm not your type – I'm all Pears soap and Marks and Spark's knickers. Merle's much more your sort. Never used soap in her life, and probably doesn't even wear knickers.'

'I wouldn't know,' Dempsey lied. 'Anyway, shall we give it a whirl, Makepeace old bean? I think it's about time.'

She nodded to him and he quietly unlocked the

bedroom door and led the way out onto the landing and up the next flight of stairs to Merle's bedroom.

They moved silently on the thick Wilton carpet and the only noise they were both conscious of was their own heartbeat. Outside the door they stopped; the house was still, but from inside the room Dempsey could hear a rustling noise – as if someone was dressing in a hurry. He looked at Makepeace and winked.

'Okay?' he whispered, and she nodded.

Dempsey tried the door handle, firmly but gently, and as the knob turned he opened the door and walked into the room.

Merle was sat at her dressing table; she was already dressed, in her black outfit. Her head was bent forward as she fixed the black hat and veil in place with a long hat pin. Dempsey looked about the room, and in a fraction of a second he had registered the assortment of whips on a rack on one wall, a set of stocks by the side of a large bed, and the thick leather straps on each corner of the bed. It looked like a whore's workshop.

Dempsey moved into the centre of the room and felt nausea sweep over him. Merle turned on her stool and smiled, and then saw Makepeace standing in the doorway behind Dempsey.

'What's this?' she cried and stood up, recognizing Makepeace from the warehouse.

'This?' Dempsey jerked his thumb over his shoulder towards Makepeace. 'This is Detective Sergeant Harriet Makepeace, my partner. Oh, and by the way, my name's Dempsey, not Schwartz.'

'You bastard.' Merle's voice seemed to change and drop about an octave, and she ripped the hat pin from her hair, kicked off her high heels and crouched low on the carpet.

'Watch out!' cried Makepeace, and drew her revolver. Dempsey saw her gun from the corner of his eye and held up a hand to Makepeace.

'Okay, Harry – I think I can handle this big cat in my own way.' Merle came for him fast, screaming like a banshee, holding the hat pin low in her fist, ready to bring it up fast into Dempsey's gut.

Dempsey held his ground for a second, and then sidestepped slightly, wrong footing Merle, and as she adjusted for the change in direction, against every chivalrous instinct, he clenched his fist and delivered a copybook right cross very accurately and with all his power, to her jaw.

The hat pin ripped into his jacket and Merle's neck snapped back, as the blow dislocated her lower jaw-bone, her knees buckled and she collapsed back onto her bed.

'Jesus Christ!' Dempsey said, as he regained his breath and looked down at Merle. The black skirt had rucked up at waist height, revealing a suspender belt and black stockings, and as Makepeace had surmised earlier, no knickers. The jet-black hairpiece lay on the floor with the veil and hat, and Merle's head was clean-shaven and ugly.

'You son-of-a-bitch.' Dempsey shuddered as he remembered how close he'd come to winding up in bed with Merle, and he heard the intake of breath from Makepeace as she stood behind him and looked at the limp penis beneath the rumpled skirt.

'Well, at least he wasn't Jewish, if that's any consolation.' She looked up at Dempsey's face and saw the horror behind his eyes. 'And I think you've broken his jaw.'

CHAPTER TEN

Like all good successful Jewish boys, Samuel Lipman lived in Highgate. Sammy was, like his father and his uncle, an accountant, and although he'd married a gentile girl much against his father's wishes, he was still the apple of his father's eye. This was in part due to the prompt and obliging way his daughter-in-law had delivered a grandson to him, but also to his son Sammy's ability to succeed in the business of making a profit, by running rings around the tax laws for, and on behalf of, his wealthy showbiz clients.

'Sammy,' he'd say, 'did you have a good month?' and Sammy would nod.

'Yes, father – better than last month, but not as good as next, eh?'

Old man Solomon Lipman would chuckle and nod his head.

'And how's Solomon, my little grandson? Is he walking yet?'

'Not yet father, but he's cut his first tooth.'

'That's good, that's good. And how's your wife?' Solomon always referred to his son's wife as 'the wife' and never by her Christian name.

'Elizabeth?' Sammy would always prompt.

'Yes?' His father would always reply, never falling into the trap. 'Yes, how is she?'

'She's fine – it's her birthday on Sunday,' he said on this occasion. If he told him it would take about four hours before the whole family knew, including Elizabeth.

'It's a surprise, Dad,' and he left it at that.

Sammy got up early on the morning of his wife's

123

birthday, made some tea, woke the au pair, and took two cups of tea back to bed.

Elizabeth looked at the tea and then at the clock, and buried her head in the pillows. 'Sammy, it's six-thirty and a Sunday.'

Sammy smiled and slipped back into bed. 'Happy Birthday darling,' he whispered and attempted a clumsy caress. She pushed his hand away and leant on one elbow.

'Sammy!' she said, rubbing the sleep from her eyes, wishing she hadn't drunk as much at her husband's cousin's Barmitzvah the day before. 'It's too early for birthday treats, you men are all the same, a quick grope and you think that's it.' She sipped at the tea and smiled at Sammy, as if she'd enjoyed the mild scolding that she'd given him. 'Anyway, why so early? Doesn't even a gentile girl get to lie in on her birthday?'

'Not today,' Sammy said. 'Today's a full programme of treats and surprises – and no more gropes,' he added as an afterthought, 'well, not until later maybe.'

'Oh!' She sat up in bed and smoothed down the duvet cover, anticipating a shower of presents. 'That's nice.'

'But first you get dressed,' Sammy instructed, 'then we get a cab.'

'A cab! What about little Solomon?'

'Little Solomon is to spend the day with Ingrid, that's all fixed. Don't worry about your precious son. All you have to do is to pray for fine weather. First you get dressed, I'll ring for the cab now,' and he picked up the phone by the bed and dialled a number. Elizabeth reluctantly got out of bed and finished her cup of tea. She knew about Sammy's treats and surprises and that the best thing to do was just to follow instructions and play the game.

'Hello – I'd like a taxi, please – yes, right away. It's to go to Claridges,' and he gave their Highgate address and hung up.

'Claridges!' echoed Elizabeth. 'What for?'

Sammy jumped out of bed and grinned like a schoolboy. 'Breakfast,' he said. 'The taxi will be here in ten minutes, so get a move on.'

The Rolls-Royce stopped outside No. 4 Hanover Terrace and Davros got out. He looked shifty, and stood by the car for some minutes before opening the boot and lifting out two heavy aluminium suitcases. He closed the boot and carried the two cases to the front door of the house. Dempsey opened the door as he approached and Davros went quickly inside. Dempsey closed the door as a lone jogger ran past the house. He was wearing a Walkman portable radio underneath a woollen bobble hat and a throat mike.

'Hello Charlie seven. The cargo has arrived at the house. Over.'

'Charlie seven, Roger. Move off and keep moving. Out.'

Dempsey followed Davros into the dining room and took one of the cases. He placed it on the D-ended table and tried to open it.

'You got the keys, Davros?'

'Sure I have the keys.'

'Well open the goddamn case, I gotta check the stuff.'

Davros pulled the keys from his pocket and threw them onto the table contemptuously. 'Open it yourself.'

Dempsey shrugged and unlocked the case. Inside were small black plastic envelopes, all heat-sealed, all weighing two ounces precisely. Dempsey took one from the centre of the case and broke open the seal. He took a small bottle of clear liquid from his pocket which had been part of Schwartz's luggage, and emptied a pinch of the powder into the liquid. He replaced the screwtop, shook the bottle and grinned greedily at Davros when the liquid turned bright purple.

'Grade four – very high quality. Our customers will be pleased, Davros, and those boys of yours in Kilburn, they've done a good job.'

Davros grunted and lifted the other suitcase onto the

125

table, and Dempsey repeated the test, and then snapped, 'Did you count 'em?'

Davros frowned. 'No.'

'You what? You didn't count 'em? You stupid or something?'

The big man shifted uneasily. He didn't like being spoken to like that, but the American was a professional – maybe he should have double-checked.

'I'll count them now,' he said sullenly, 'we have time.'

'You do that buster – I'll go and see if Merle's ready to go, then we better get our asses outta here and down to the docks.' Dempsey left the big man reluctantly counting the packets of heroin and hoped that by the time he'd finished it, it would be time to go. He couldn't risk any close contact between Davros and Merle or the game would be well and truly up. He went up the stairs quickly and knocked on the bedroom door.

'Merle, can I come in?' and without waiting for a reply, he opened the door and went into the bedroom and closed the door quietly behind him. Merle was in front of the mirror making the final adjustments to the hairpiece, the hat and the veil. Dempsey caught his breath momentarily and stared as she stood up, lowered the veil and turned round.

'How do I look, Schwartz?'

'Makepeace, you look just great,' he said and she twirled in front of the looking glass, inspecting the mirror image of Merle with a sense of satisfaction and trepidation.

'Will I do, d'you think?'

'As long as that ape Davros doesn't get too close. You had me fooled when I came through the door – but you'd better put some of that perfume on.'

'What are we going to do with your – friend?' She nodded towards Merle who was gagged and secured to the bed with the thick leather straps at each corner. He was lying spread-eagled and naked, and in order to

126

retain a sense of decorum, Dempsey had placed a large straw hat over his crutch and stuck a feather in the top of the hat.

'I guess the boys'll be crawling all over this place about thirty seconds after we leave – I don't think we need worry about Miss Merle, but I guess I'll leave them a note.' He took a lipstick from the dressing table and stood over Merle who was shaking with fear. 'Hold still sister – this won't hurt a bit,' and he wrote on the flat, hairless chest: 'Spikings is a fag. Long live Spikings'.

He looked down at the pathetic creature and shook his head. 'When you get outta the slammer pal, if you ain't too old, that is, you should take a trip over to the rotten Apple – 43rd Street's crawling with perverts like you, I pick 'em off the sidewalk every night like dead cats,' and he turned to Makepeace as he heard the first footfall on the staircase below.

'C'mon sweetheart – it's showtime,' and he opened the door and ushered her out onto the landing, closed the door and locked it, putting the key in his pocket. 'Hey Davros,' he called down the stairwell, 'are you all through counting?'

'All finished, all correct. Is Merle ready?' His deep voice boomed up the staircase and Dempsey looked at Makepeace and winked.

'Yeah. We're coming down now, start getting the stuff into the car, will you.'

He stopped walking up the stairs when he saw Makepeace wave him back and indicate that he get on with the job. Dempsey held his breath, hoping that she wasn't going to try and say anything, but he turned without a word and went back to the dining room.

Dempsey took Makepeace by the arm. 'Leave the Academy Awards till later, Makepeace – you're making me nervous. Let's get in the car. C'mon,' and they walked down the last flight of stairs and out into the cold morning.

'Hello Charlie seven, Dempsey's leaving with the

woman, and the big Greek is following with two suitcases. Over.'

'Charlie seven. Pull back now. Out.'

Spikings narrowed his eyes against the wind and peered over the edge of the flat roof of the Tower Hotel that overlooked St. Katharine's dock and Drew's Wharf. He raised a pair of binoculars to his eyes, and swept the dock area and the approach to the wharf. In all he could identify eight of his men, hidden among the buildings and parked cars surrounding the wharf. Morris was at his side, talking quietly into a handset.

'Hello Charlie two and three – move in closer now, but on no account allow yourselves to be seen. The two orientals are at the river side of the wharf, but they may move back. Keep your frequency open at all times. Over.'

Inside the warehouse that overlooked the wharf the two Koreans lay still, watching and waiting for the arrival of Lei Shan. They smoked as they waited in their private silent world, like two yellow lizards on a rock, and one of them rubbed the flat bridge of his nose and could feel the bone move slightly and he remembered the face of the blonde girl who yesterday had drop-kicked him so neatly.

The tide was on the flood and they watched as the level of the river rose up the heavy wooden platform of the wharf. It was a very high tide, and further down the estuary the control room of the Thames Barrier was watching carefully for a change in wind direction. The river looked grey and huge and powerful as it pushed at the crumbling banks of London's old dockland, some parts a hundred years old or more.

It was weak, watery sunlight that reflected off the moving band of water, as it poured past Tower Bridge on its way to Teddington Lock. Spikings looked down at the river and from his observation point could see to his right the river bend past Cannon Street Station and the Savoy Hotel and then up to Big Ben and the Houses of Parliament, and below him the Tower of London, empty now of its tourists who scamper about its old battlements in summer and drop ice-cream wrappers off the edge of the Bloody Tower and Traitor's Gate.

There was an old Thames sailing barge called *Daphne* which was moored alongside Tower Pier, and as he watched he saw a van pull up, and then for several minutes he observed the driver of the van unload cases of wine and champagne from the van onto the barge.

'Someone's gonna have a party today, Morris,' he nodded down to the pier. 'They've got enough booze aboard to last our department for a week.'

Morris took the binoculars from the boss and focused onto the deck of the barge. 'Probably some Hooray Henrys from Sloane Square, guv, off on a jolly to Burnham-on-Crouch,' he said, imitating a Sloane Ranger remarkably well for a black Scotsman. 'They'll be off soon I wouldn't wonder.'

'Oh yeah. Why d'you say that then? I didn't know you were a sailing man, Morris.'

'It's about half an hour off high tide, guv. They'll cast off and get underway when there's slack water and have the ebb tide with them all the way down.' As he spoke the first of a succession of taxis dropped off clutches of giggling young men and women, and Morris watched as they clambered aboard the old barge with about as much respect for the old girl as a borstal day trip at a fun fair.

The Rolls-Royce moved into London Wall, passing between the tall impersonal buildings of the City. Dempsey sat in the back with Makepeace and Davros drove. From behind her veil, Makepeace could see the reflection of the big Greek in his rear view mirror, and she watched his face intently for any hint of suspicion. Dempsey kept his eyes to the front and the three of them shared an eerie silence, broken only by the soft hiss of the air conditioning unit. Dempsey looked at his watch, and as they turned right into Moorgate he saw the taxi that had been with them since Regent's Park halfway down London Wall. The taxi turned left and a small Austin 1300 took its place.

'They're good,' thought Dempsey, and he hoped that S.I.10 were as good at a shoot-out as they were at keeping a tail. He had that feeling in the pit of his stomach that everything was about to come together pretty soon and, like most times, nobody could predict how it would turn out. One thing was for sure – there would be death on the banks of the Thames within the next hour – that he would put money on, and Dempsey only bet on certainties.

He looked at Makepeace out of the corner of his eye. He felt he ought to break the silence that had been observed ever since they'd left Hanover Terrace.

'Don't be nervous,' he said, and patted the back of her hand. 'If there are no problems we'll be outta here and on our way to Dover in under an hour. By this time tomorrow we'll be in Zurich, the money will be in the bank, I can pay you off and we'll all be home free. What d'you say, Davros ol' buddy . . .' and he slapped the fat man's shoulder. 'What you gonna do with your share, eh?' The big man shrugged and tried not to answer. He didn't like the American and if the job had not been clearly the most important priority, he'd have torn him limb from limb.

Davros and Merle had been lovers – he had known Merle for many years – since 1974 when they both had been engaged to perform, in different ways, at a gay party given by a government minister in a country house in Hertfordshire. But since then Merle had become rather grand and although their mutual needs still remained very much a common bond, the frequency of those needs became a rare occurrence. Merle used Davros, holding their bizarre sexual appetite aloft, like a phallic carrot that occasionally dangled within reach, and when it happened, Merle used the

130

onslaught as a punishment for the torment that Davros endured during his long periods of celibacy. But in recent months the relationship between them had become even more strained, and Merle had flirted deliberately, so Davros thought, in front of him, somehow in order to hurt him. He looked at her in the mirror and caught the look from Dempsey. He gripped the wheel tighter and made a vow to himself to dispose of the American wheeler and dealer whenever the opportunity arose, after the deal had been done.

Makepeace caught the look from Davros and thanked God for the veil. She pushed the black kid gloves harder onto her fingers, and felt the sweat on the palms of her hands stick to the gloves.

Five minutes later the Rolls stopped outside the entrance to the warehouse behind Drew's Wharf. Davros looked at Dempsey for some indication of where to put the car.

'Park it inside – I'll open the doors. Merle, you give me a hand. Stay here, Davros,' and Dempsey got out of the car, ran round and opened the door for Makepeace before Davros could do as he usually did, and help Merle out of the car.

'C'mon, Merle.' He was whispering now, and looking shiftily about him. 'Let's go find Tweedle-dum and Tweedle-dee,' and he hurried her away from the car. 'Keep away from the Korean bastards if you can, they can smell smoke about a mile away.'

'But I don't smoke,' she hissed back at him.

'No – but Merle does.'

'Oh!' she said, and then understood.

Dempsey swung the two old paint-flaked maroon doors open, and looked inside the warehouse. It was dirty and he guessed unused for forty years or so. The building seemed sound enough, but it stank of the damp of the river, and the iron supports that ran right up to the roof were wet to the touch. Dempsey shivered and blinked until his eyes became accustomed to the half-light. Makepeace was standing by his side, she was very close – he guessed because she was scared shitless – and as he touched her arm to give her a little confidence, he saw a slight movement at the other end of the building. He froze momentarily and then waved at the two Koreans, who silently came towards them out of the shadows.

CHAPTER ELEVEN

The small Mercury speed-boat skimmed along the brimming surface of the river, coming towards Tower Bridge from the east. It hugged the north side of the river, as if seeking as much cover from the shadows of the tall unused buildings, and then, as it neared the entrance to Drew's Wharf, Serge cut the throttle and the small craft sank into the water as the bow came off the plane.

Lei Shan stood up in the boat and pointed to a set of wooden steps that led up to the hard-standing next to the warehouse. 'Over there,' she snapped.

Serge nodded and eased the throttle open slightly and brought the small craft alongside, held it momentarily against what was left of the flood tide, and then attached a line to an iron ring in the concrete.

Behind her were two men; they sat sullenly in the back of the boat, and across their knees rested Heckler and Koch machine pistols. Lei Shan checked her watch.

'They will be there now, remember when we have completed the exchange, the American must die – leave the girl and the Greek, I have no quarrel with them. And let them take the money. But Schwartz must not get away. Do you understand?' The two men nodded and both checked their weapons.

'Serge –' she turned to him and placed a hand on his shoulder – 'be ready to leave quickly.'

He nodded, and tapped the end of the line that was secured to the ring. 'It is a slip-knot, there will be no delay and I shall keep the engine running.'

She climbed the wooden ladder onto the hard-standing and waited for the other two. Both of them carried two identical cases, and as they stood together the Koreans suddenly opened the double doors that led into the long empty warehouse. The two gunmen slipped the machine pistols into the firing position, but Lei Shan put up her hands.

'Easy. We don't want any mistakes now, just keep your eyes open.' She looked into the gloom of the warehouse and saw Dempsey and Makepeace at the other end of the cluttered brick floor. Behind them stood the huge figure of Davros carrying the two aluminium cases containing the heroin. 'Tell your two Korean dogs to fall back behind you.'

Lei Shan's command was strong and clear, and the two men looked back for instruction.

Makepeace beckoned slowly with one finger. It was exactly as Merle would have done and the two Koreans obediently withdrew into the building until they stood behind Davros.

Lei Shan moved slowly into the building, and from where Dempsey stood their figures were black silhouettes for a few seconds until they came out of the sunlight into the shadows. In front of them they'd arranged two large tea-chests, and as Lei Shan's party approached, Dempsey waved Davros forward. The approaching party stopped as soon as Davros began to move, and not until he'd put the cases on the tea-chests, opened them both and retired behind Dempsey and Makepeace did Lei Shan instruct one of her gunmen to do likewise.

No one moved until the man returned to his position behind Lei Shan, and then she stepped forward and spoke to Dempsey.

'One million dollars in each case, in used notes of mixed denomination, non-sequential.' She paused. 'Less fifty thousand, as agreed by us on the telephone yesterday, Mr Schwartz.'

There was a pause and Dempsey wondered what next. He had his Magnum, with six ·44 calibre rounds, and Makepeace had her issue ·38. No match for two Heckler and Koch G11 machine pistols with a cyclic rate of fire of two thousand rounds a minute, fired in three-second bursts.

Dempsey adjusted his weight onto his left foot and popped a stick of chewing gum into his mouth in an attempt to prevent his teeth from chattering.

'Merle, check the dough,' and he nodded at Makepeace, and raised his voice to Lei Shan. 'You wanna check the stuff?'

Lei Shan came closer and looked hard into Dempsey's eyes – he wasn't quite what she'd expected. His colouring and age were as she'd remembered, and his hair was similar, but his eyes seemed kinder than she'd remembered.

'I don't think that will be necessary, Mr Schwartz, as the checking of money is also unnecessary. But if you insist, it's your privilege.'

Davros moved forward of Dempsey and watched over Makepeace's shoulder, as she inspected the money. Her gloves were making the checking look clumsy, and she took them off in order to flick through the piles of dollars.

Lei Shan, oblivious to their interest in the money, was staring at Dempsey and Dempsey was looking with some trepidation at Davros. There was, for a brief moment, only the sound of Makepeace flicking through the small, neat piles of money, like a professional with a new deck of cards, and then suddenly Davros checked his breathing and for an instant he stood very still. He looked at the short, clipped fingernails that shuffled their way through the money and Dempsey's heart skipped a beat and he reached for his gun.

'What's this!' roared the Greek, and in one swift movement he ripped at the hat and veil and the long blonde hair fell onto Makepeace's shoulders. Dempsey's eyes flicked in the direction of the boys with the Heckler and Koches and they weren't quite so quick. Makepeace stood for a second, her eyes wide open, like a rabbit in the headlights of a car, not knowing what to do.

135

'Okay – everybody freeze!' Dempsey yelled at the top of his voice, conscious that the two Koreans were behind him and almost expecting to feel the thudding blow at the base of the neck. He turned slightly and saw one of them dive for cover behind a pile of old boxes. He turned back again and squeezed his first round at the heavy back of one of Lei Shan's gunmen. He buckled as the round hit his thigh, but he remained standing and brought his gun up to the shoulder. Dempsey adjusted his aim and fired again. The man screamed and pitched back onto the floor, his finger squeezing the trigger and the 4·7 mm rounds sprayed the ceiling, covering everything in plaster and pieces of flying concrete.

Makepeace drew her ·38, but before she could use it, Davros grabbed the revolver from her grasp and held her in a vice-like grip to his body. The side door of the warehouse burst open and suddenly the air was filled with fresh cordite and screamed instructions. Spikings was first through the door, and Morris was close on his governor's heels. Four men came through from the river side and two more came from the other end of the warehouse. Lei Shan was the quickest to react, and she dodged through the side door that Spikings had come from and ran down the side of the building to the front of the wharf. Morris loosed off two quick shots at her as she ran away, and she stumbled and nearly fell, but regained her balance and carried on.

Dempsey felt something behind him, he didn't know what, but as he turned he saw one of the Koreans, as if in flight, coming for him. He fired two shots at the approaching yellow head, and it split open like a water melon and he felt the warm splashes of blood and brain on his face as the dead man hit him. Both he and the Korean crashed to the ground together and as he tried to scramble to his feet he heard the voice of Davros above the noise.

'If anybody moves, the woman dies.' Dempsey shook the Korean from him and stood up. Davros had

Makepeace in a head-lock, her own gun held to her head and he had her almost lifted off the ground by her neck.

'Dempsey – drop it.'

It was Spikings. He'd lowered his gun and so had Morris.

'Dempsey – put your gun down. Immediately!'

Dempsey slowly lowered his Magnum to the floor.

'Now drop it.' Dempsey looked at Spikings.

'Drop it, Dempsey – that's an order.' Dempsey let the heavy gun drop onto the brickwork.

Davros backed away, hauling Makepeace after him, like a doll. 'If anyone tries to stop me, she dies, right here and now.' And then to Dempsey, 'Where is Merle?'

Dempsey's eyes narrowed. 'By now he's in the slammer I guess.'

'You bastard!' and there were tears in Davros's eyes. 'You bastard!'

Dempsey said nothing; he just looked at the frightened eyes of his partner and felt helpless.

Davros jerked his head to the remaining Korean. 'Get the car – now!' The man hesitated and then ran for the Rolls.

Spikings was breathing hard, and he was scared. Detective Sergeant Harriet Makepeace was one he really didn't want to have wasted on a job like this.

'Leave her be,' he said gruffly. 'Leave her be, and I guarantee a safe passage for you out of here.'

Davros laughed. 'You crazy! She stops with me. For as long as need be. Dead or alive.'

And he turned to Dempsey. 'You, whoever you are, get the money – put it in the boot of the car.'

Dempsey hesitated.

'Get it now!' and he jerked at Makepeace's neck savagely.

Dempsey walked slowly to the tea-chests where the opened cases lay. He closed them both and turned, as the Rolls backed into the open end of the warehouse.

137

He walked to the boot, put down the cases and opened the boot. Davros had hauled Makepeace to the side of the car and had opened the rear door. Dempsey threw the two cases of money in the boot and closed it with a bang, and then he looked at Davros.

'You hurt her and I'll kill you. Y'understand?'

Davros pushed her roughly into the back of the car and got in after her.

'Go!' he yelled at the Korean, and the car moved quickly out of the warehouse.

At the same time Lei Shan dropped into the boat, clutching at her bloody upper arm.

'Go – quickly!' She snapped the command at Serge through clenched teeth, as she fought the pain in the torn flesh. 'Go, damn you. Go!'

Serge slipped the rope from the cleat on the boat bulkhead, and pushed the throttle open. The stern of the boat churned as the prop bit into the water and the small boat slowly accelerated and then lifted onto a plane, as the slack water of high tide pulled at the hull like treacle.

Dempsey watched helplessly as the big car's tyres spun for a moment on the wet cobbles, and then, gathering speed, turned right. The back end of the car slid on the road and crashed into a parked car as the Korean over-corrected for the skid. Dempsey snatched his Magnum from the ground, and followed the Rolls.

'Dempsey!' Spikings yelled at him. 'Don't try anything. He'll kill her!'

Dempsey watched the Rolls as it see-sawed its way up the narrow road that led to East Smithfield, and for an instant he saw the white, frightened face of his partner in the rear window, as she grappled helplessly with Davros. He looked to his left and saw the powder blue ironwork of Tower Bridge and he mentally flipped a coin and then ran towards the bridge. When the Rolls got to East Smithfield it could either go left or right. Right went to Wapping and the East End. Left would bring it back towards the City and the bridge. The original plan had been to complete the exchange and then make for Dover, pick up the midday ferry to Calais and then drive flat out for Switzerland. Dempsey took a chance; he gambled everything on the Rolls taking the next left over Tower Bridge, and he ran as he'd never run before.

Sammy Lipman helped Elizabeth from the taxi and took her arm. She tottered a little and then stood still, unsure of her balance, due in part to the Buck's Fizz at Claridges, the only thing to drink with birthday kedgeree so Sammy said, and the fact that she was blindfold. Sammy's little surprise.

He paid off the cab, turned Elizabeth round to face the pier and then took off her blindfold.

'Happy birthday, darling,' he said. She blinked and then saw the sailing barge and a banner saying 'Happy Birthday' and all her friends lining the gangway and aboard the barge.

'Oh Sammy!' she said and hugged her husband, and was very happy she'd decided to marry this kind Jewish man. Much against her mother's wishes.

The barge slipped its mooring, the skipper dropped the red gaff sail and unfurled the jib and the old Stuart Turner diesel engine throbbed below the deck and eased the barge out into mid-stream. Sammy put his arm round her waist and pulled her to him.

'We're going all the way down to Whitstable, and then we get off, have an oyster lunch and get into a coach for a pub-crawl back to London, if we're still standing that is. But first . . .'

Dempsey's lungs felt as though they would burst, and the muscles in his legs were losing all their power. He ran on, through St Katharine's Dock, and he felt the iron red bridge flex slightly as he ran over the lock that connected the dock with the river. An elderly couple stopped in amazement as he ran past, his face in pain with the effort of running and the ·44 Magnum held firmly in his right hand, but Dempsey didn't even see them. He concentrated on maintaining his speed, because he knew that if he'd made the right decision, there wouldn't be much room for error, and the success of his attempt would depend entirely on how quickly he could get onto the bridge.

He ran behind the Tower Hotel, past the hotel loading bay and on to the stone steps that led up onto the approach to Tower Bridge. The steps were steep, and he felt the strength in his legs dwindle as he stopped halfway up, and using his hands as well as his legs, almost crawled up the last few steps on all fours. He fell onto the pavement at the top, and knelt for a few seconds, desperately pulling the air back into his lungs. His legs were shaking with the effort and at first he found it difficult to stand. All he could see were spots racing before his eyes. He looked up and as he did so he heard the squeal of tyres and then he saw the Rolls slew round the corner from East Smithfield and power towards him.

Automatically he checked the chamber in the Magnum. There were two rounds left and he reached into his jacket and grabbed at the loose rounds in his pocket. Keeping an eye on the approaching car, he started to clumsily thumb the big rounds into the empty chambers; some dropped onto the road, some went in. He didn't know how many. The Rolls was getting closer now and Dempsey could see the Korean with the broken nose at the wheel of the car and in the back he could make out the bulky outline of Davros and the blonde hair of Makepeace.

Dempsey stepped out into the middle of the road, and held the Magnum in front of him with both hands. His chest was still heaving and the heavy handgun waved around the target of the approaching car. Somewhere in the distance Dempsey heard the wail of a police siren and then behind him he heard a long low blast of a river boat. He snapped a shot at the Rolls,

140

the Magnum kicked violently in his hands, and he saw the strike on the vertical chrome struts of the radiator. He fired again and the windscreen shattered on the empty passenger side; the car swerved dangerously across the road and reduced speed.

Two shots gone and Dempsey couldn't remember how many more he'd managed to load into the chamber. Three maybe, or was it two, he didn't know. Then suddenly he was aware of a movement, but he seemed to feel it through his feet. He looked quickly behind him and saw that a red and white barrier had dropped across the road and that the bridge was about to open.

In the control room on the east side of the North Buttress, the officer of the watch had acknowledged the request from the fully-rigged Thames sailing barge *Daphne*. Having checked in the day log when he took over the watch at 08.00 hrs, and noted the request for the bridge to be opened at high water for a fully rigged barge to go downstream, he'd rung the Bridge Commander at his private flat in Knightsbridge, asking why it was necessary. Why couldn't they lower the mast and go down under power?

'They want to go down under sail, written request with forty-eight hours' notice I'm afraid. So we're obliged,' and the Commander had hung up, not appreciating the early Sunday interruption.

The massive iron locking bolts withdrew in the centre and at the fulcrum of the road bridge, and then the two sections began to move through the 90° arc.

Sammy Lipman eased the cork from the magnum of Bolinger at the first sign of a gap in the bridge and whispered into Elizabeth's ear.

'They're opening the bridge for you doll, as a salute to your old age.' She looked up at Sammy and the cork from the Bolinger popped and everybody clapped.

Dempsey fired two more rounds into the oncoming windscreen of the Rolls and suddenly the front wheels of the car locked and it skidded to a halt, finally coming to rest on the kerb only feet from Dempsey. The Korean leapt from the car and Dempsey saw the tell-tale patch of blood that was already seeping fast from his left shoulder. He ran at Dempsey without any regard for the wound in his shoulder and Dempsey momentarily saw the glazed look in the man's eyes, and he knew he was in shock and working only on instinct. Dempsey side-stepped and steadied himself on the cast-iron parapet of the bridge, and as the Korean came at him he kicked viciously at the man's crutch.

The toe-cap of his shoe dug deep into the soft nether regions of the Korean and found its mark. The man slithered to his knees and let out a shrill scream of pain. Dempsey brought his knee up fast, under the man's chin, and he saw the yellow teeth disintegrate on one another. He turned and Davros had his arm around Makepeace's throat and had dragged her from the car. He held her against him for protection and behind him he could hear the approaching sirens of the police cars that had been standing by as back-up for Spikings.

Davros moved fast, the only way there was, and dragging Makepeace after him he went through the open door that led into the control room of the North Tower.

Dempsey followed and as he went through the doorway, he saw the black spiral iron steps that led down into the bascule chamber, and he saw Davros almost carrying Makepeace like a rag doll, down the echoing steps into the cold wet brickwork of the tower. He fired a wild shot at Dempsey which ricocheted off the iron staircase and the sound of the shot echoed down into the tower.

Dempsey's chest heaved again with fear and exhaustion, and he half stumbled, half fell down the steps, almost dropping his own gun. He regained his balance and stopped for a second, and saw Davros reach an opening in the brickwork large enough to allow him access. He loosed off another round at Dempsey and disappeared into the opening, pulling Makepeace behind him.

Dempsey, throwing all caution to the wind, leapt the last few steps and stood in the opening in the brick-work. Inside was a huge brick chamber, shaped like a quadrant. He could see a sheer wall on his left and right, and above his head he saw from the dim glow from two bulkhead lights, the counterbalance weight. The weight had the complete width of the chamber and was pivoted at the fulcrum of the bridge which was at the top of the wall to his left, and as the bridge opened in celebration of Elizabeth's birthday, so the chamber got smaller and smaller.

Davros and Makepeace were well inside the floor of the chamber and as Dempsey peered into the gloom he saw the bright stab of the third round from Davros, and his ears hurt with the deafening reverberation of the explosion in such a confined space. Two feet above his head he felt the impact of the ·38 calibre round as it embedded into the old soft Victorian brickwork.

The floor of the chamber dropped away in a series of steps, curving down until it finished at the foot of a vertical retaining wall. Davros was halfway down when he lost his footing and stumbled. Momentarily he released his hold on Makepeace and she fought like a tigress and managed to free herself from his grasp. Dempsey lunged down the curving steps and flew at Davros as he desperately tried to regain his balance, knowing full well that he was no match for the huge Greek on anything like equal terms. He smashed at the big man's face with the heel of the Magnum and the blow glanced off the side of his temple. Davros cried out with pain and the cry echoed in the diminishing brick cavern.

Makepeace looked up at the roof of the chamber and saw that the counterbalance weight was halfway through its 90° arc, and had already passed the opening that had let them into the chamber. There was no way

143

out and with every second the counterbalance weight came lower and lower until it would stop hard against the vertical wall, when the bridge would be fully open.

She saw the relentless sweep of the huge iron weight that, her fifth-form physics in the schoolgirl part of her memory told her, had to be as heavy as the road bridge it was lifting. For that second she watched mesmerized as the edge of the weight swept down, missing the brick steps by only fractions of an inch, with not enough space to let a rat escape. Automatically she backed away from it towards the wall. She was terrified.

Davros was on his knees but had Dempsey in a bear grip that was quite impossible to break, and he could feel what little breath he had left in his lungs being crushed out, and as his vision began to blur, he looked up just in time to see the moving counterbalance strike Davros from behind, sweeping them both down into the bottom of the brick arc like lemmings off a cliff. Davros let go and the two men sprawled on the wet, slimy floor. Dempsey's grip on the Magnum failed and he heard it clatter somewhere to his left. He scrambled to his feet a fraction before the Greek and as he did so he looked at Makepeace. In the gloom he saw her flattened against the brick wall and he saw that the moving counterbalance was about to move past the two dim bulkhead lights on the side walls, and as soon as that happened their shrinking chamber would be plunged into total darkness.

'Get on the wall!' Makepeace screamed at Dempsey, and he hurled himself at the brickwork and pressed himself to it like a limpet. The weight was three feet away, the lights disappeared and then there was absolute darkness.

Outside in the sunlight, the big, square locking bolts slid into place with a clunk. The bridge was in the fully open position and the sailing barge *Daphne*, to the strains of 'Happy Birthday, dear Elizabeth – Happy Birthday to you' slid through and began its journey in search of Whitstable oysters. From inside the bascule chamber there was a sickening crunching sound, and then total silence.

The wind picked up and filled the red sails of the *Daphne*, the tide began to ebb on its twice-daily rush for the North Sea, and the barge soon disappeared from view on her way to Greenwich and beyond. The locking bolts withdrew and silently the massive bridge began to close, and as the counterbalance weight pulled away from the wall, Dempsey let out the longest breath he'd ever held. His hands had been pressed hard on the cold wet rusty metal face of the weight, as instinctively, at the last moment, he'd protected his head from the unstoppable mass of iron, and then suddenly the huge wall of metal pulled back in the pitch darkness and he felt space and air in front of him again.

A second later, in its upward arc to the roof of the bascule chamber, it passed the two bulkhead lights, and he looked up at the receding weight and then to his left along the wall. Makepeace was standing flat on the wall. She looked very frightened and her face was like a white death mask in the half-light of the chamber. Dempsey spotted the glint of his Magnum on the wet brick floor and he bent slowly to retrieve it. As he did so he saw Davros. He lay sprawled on the last step of the chamber floor – crushed beyond all recognition. Part of his clothes had been ripped from his body in great chunks, and Dempsey could see bone and guts as though he'd been through a combine harvester; and blood, lots of blood.

'Oh my God,' he said softly, and moved along the wall to Makepeace. 'Don't look honey,' he said, and put himself between her and the Greek remains. 'Let's get the hell outta here.'

They slowly climbed the brick steps up to the opening in the side wall, and as they got there, shaking and out of breath, Spikings ran down the iron staircase with Morris close behind.

'Is she all right?'

Dempsey looked at Gordon Spikings and nodded. 'It's just a passing crush,' and he continued awkwardly up the staircase as she held on to him very tightly.

Spikings looked down into the chamber and then up at the counterbalance as it reached the end of its return traverse and he heard the locking bolts slide into place. He looked down again at the mess that was Davros and then at Morris, and he said quietly, 'Fuckin' hell, Morris.'

CHAPTER TWELVE

Ed Zukko's eyes creaked open, and he snatched angrily at the jangle by his bed. 'Zukko? Who ever it is – it'd better be good.' He hauled himself up on one elbow and blinked at his watch as he heard the familiar voice of Gordon Spikings.

'Ed – sorry to wake you again old son, but if it's any consolation, I haven't had any shut-eye at all since we last spoke.'

'That's absolutely no importance to me, Gordon, you asshole – what gives?'

'We got them all except the Chinese girl and a minion – they gave us the slip when the shit hit the fan but all the rest are in the bag.'

'That's good, Gordon – how did Dempsey make out?'

'He did well – he's a good cop. I think I like him.'

'You do?' There was a pause. 'Tell you what, Gordon, you can keep him, for a while anyway. He still ain't the most popular cop in the 43rd Precinct, so if you want him, you can have him.'

Spikings sniffed hard, and looked across his office at Dempsey. 'I'd rather assumed that he'd escort Schwartz back to you.'

Zukko rubbed his eyes and yawned as if indifferent to any future arrangements. All he wanted to do was to go back to sleep. 'Just put the asshole on the next 747, he don't need no escort – he ain't exactly gonna get off. We'll meet him just as soon as the wheels touch down. Don't worry, Gordon, old buddy, just do it.'

'There is a suggestion, Dempsey, that if you would like to stay here for a bit, just to help us out that is, then you can.'

Dempsey shrugged and looked at Makepeace. 'I'd

147

have to speak to my partner about that, sir, I ain't too sure she'd appreciate an extended stay.'

Spikings looked at Makepeace and raised an eyebrow. 'Well, 'arry? What d'you say?'

Makepeace grinned at Dempsey and shrugged, as if it didn't matter one way or the other. 'If he can stand the pace, it might be interesting – for a limited run, anyhow.'

Spikings spoke again into the telephone. 'There seems to be a reluctant willingness for him to stay on – for a bit anyway. If that's all right by you it's all right by me,' and he nodded and hung up.

'Well – that about wraps it up – unless you want to go back to Heathrow and say goodbye to your friend Schwartz, but I'm sure the airport police and the customs boys can handle him.'

Dempsey stood up with difficulty and swayed slightly. 'I'd rather watch the bastard get on the plane, sir, if it's all the same to you.'

'I think you'd be better off in bed,' and he looked at Makepeace. 'Both of you.'

Makepeace felt the colour rising in her cheeks. 'Hadn't you better rephrase that, sir? I mean, we've only just met.'

Schwartz stood between two large uniformed airport policemen. He looked smug and confident. Dempsey and Makepeace stood on the other side of the passenger jet-way that led into the main door of the TWA flight to New York and they all waited there until the last few passengers shuffled aboard, nodding with disinterest at the welcoming smiles that shone from a battery of stewardesses.

'Good evening, sir. Welcome aboard.' Dempsey nodded at the girl and ushered Schwartz into the aircraft. The smile on the girl's face extinguished like a bonfire in a thunderstorm, and she looked nervously at Dempsey.

'Mr Schwartz here is an extra passenger – he's

148

travelling alone and will be met at the other end. Can you make sure he's first off, and get your Captain to check that his reception committee is all fixed up before you open the doors. Okay?'

The professional smile returned, like wintery sunshine on a coffin lid, and she consulted the passenger manifest.

'He'll have to go first class – every other seat's occupied.'

Dempsey shrugged at the final irony. 'Lady – just get the bastard to Kennedy. It'll be his last good meal for one hell of a long time.' He turned to Schwartz. 'See you in court asshole,' and he watched as the girl showed Schwartz to an aisle seat in the forward section of the aircraft. She waited until he had sat down and then she came back to where Dempsey stood.

'He won't give you any trouble – he's too smart to try anything; just keep feeding him booze and he'll sleep all the way.'

'What a shame you're not coming too.'

'Yeah,' he said and looked at Makepeace, who was leaning on the doorway of the aircraft and registering mild disapproval. Dempsey smiled at the girl and jerked his thumb at Makepeace. 'Gotta go – my old lady's the jealous type,' and once again the smile on the girl's face faded, but somehow still left the teeth exposed.

'C'mon, Makepeace, let's go!' and he took her by the arm and led her back up the jet-way to the main terminal building.

'Don't for one minute let me cramp your style,' she said, and just for a second Dempsey picked up a note of petulance in her voice.

'Hell no – the same goes for me too,' and they both avoided any more conversation until they were out of the airport and back on the M4 into London.

Dempsey looked out of the car window at the skyline of London and he felt a strange cold isolation creep into his bones like a winter spent in Buffalo, when it was so bitter the goddamn lake froze.

'Some honeymoon that was,' he thought, and he remembered the hit-and-run, and the face of the man at the wheel of the Cadillac. He'd never forget the face of the man at the wheel of the Cadillac, never. A killer's face, framed in the clean arc of glass behind a snow covered windscreen, forever locked in Dempsey's memory. He could hear the muffled crunching of the chains on the tyres in the snow, and the racing engine and then a split-second of silence before the grill and the chrome fender and the nearside headlights smashed his new bride, tearing her hand from his, and carrying her fifty yards back up the sidewalk before she fell beneath the wheels, and the chains on the tyres and the blood in the snow.

'Why did you decide to stay on?' Makepeace said softly, almost as though she knew that he was some place else. Dempsey wiped away the beginnings of a tear, as if his eyes were just tired, and he looked away from the outside darkness.

'Time to move on I guess.' He paused. 'Time for a change, time for a new start maybe.'

She looked at him quickly and then back at the road. 'That sounds a bit like a line from a western,' she said lightly, and then wished she'd not said it. 'Sorry – didn't mean to sound trite.'

He smiled at his new English partner's tight-lipped, upper-class apology and wondered how long it would be before he'd suggest the inevitable.

'That's okay – but I'm an East Coast city boy – I ain't never rode the range.'

'I've never been to New York – is it really as violent as its reputation?'

'Oh yeah. It's violent sure enough, but hell, so is London – or had you forgotten? Big cities are much the same the world over, I guess. You get people and money all together in the same place and you got an instant recipe for violence and crime. It's human nature; it's called greed.'

She nodded. 'I suppose you're right. Apart from crimes of passion.'

'Even some of them, when you come right down to it, are caused indirectly by greed – even if it's only wanting somebody who don't belong to you. It's the same thing.'

The car drove on and their conversation continued and then got less formal, and as they came off the motorway at Hammersmith, Dempsey began to look about him, inspecting in more detail the old capital that once had been the hub of the world and now was to be his home. He didn't know for how long, but he guessed that he could quite happily hang out his stay for maybe six months. There was a lot to forget about New York, so perhaps it wasn't such a dumb idea to stay for a while.

'Which is your favourite restaurant?' Dempsey asked, suddenly remembering that he hadn't eaten since the never-to-be-forgotten dinner with Merle the night before.

'Why – is that an invitation?'

'Could be – you hungry?'

'Actually I am – but unless we go to a hotel, we might find Sunday evening a bit tricky.' She paused and looked at her watch. 'How much cash have you?'

He shrugged. 'Cash I don't have. An armful of credit cards I have.'

'Okay – then you can take me to the Connaught.'

'Is that expensive?'

'Very.'

'Have you booked, sir?' The maître d' of the Connaught looked at Dempsey in a rather grand and disapproving manner, as though he was the boy delivering the fresh bread rolls, and was late.

'Nope.'

'I'll have to consult our reservations, sir, one

moment,' and he turned and walked to the desk. Dempsey looked at Makepeace and raised an eyebrow.

'This is your favourite place?'

'Yes – the food is quite terrific,' she enthused.

'That guy who's doing the Noël Coward look-alike, does he own the place or is he just a waiter?'

'He's the head waiter – and it's probably better if you let me do the talking.'

'Listen duchess, I pick up the tab – I do the talking, okay? I know how to handle guys like him,' and he turned to face the man as he came back from the reception book. Makepeace knew what he was going to say.

'I'm afraid, sir, that it is quite impossible this evening. The restaurant is fully booked. Perhaps you'd care to make a reservation for later in the week.'

Dempsey peered past his shoulder at the restaurant which seemed less than half full. 'You got empty tables there. I can see 'em.'

'They are for residents, sir.'

'Then I'll book a room.'

The man's face remained unchanged. 'I have a feeling that all the rooms are taken. We're always very busy at the beginning of a new year. But I'll enquire.'

Dempsey stepped towards the man in a threatening manner until their faces were very close. 'Listen, buster, my friend here thinks you run the best place in town, but so far you ain't doing too good. We have just had a bad day and I don't care if you set up a table in the goddamn elevator, we're gonna eat here, y'understand?'

The maître d' coughed and looked at Makepeace who smiled sweetly.

'In which case, sir, I wonder if I could ask you to choose a necktie from a selection we have. It is a rule, you see, that diners should be wearing ties.'

Dempsey looked at Makepeace who was maintaining her sweet smile with difficulty. 'What d'you think, do I choose a tie or do we go find a McDonald's?'

'I'll choose the tie, and just for the record, I've never eaten a hamburger in my life and I don't intend to start now.' She turned to the other man. 'Is Lord Winfield in the restaurant this evening?'

'I believe his Lordship has a table at nine, but I . . .'

'I wonder if you'd ask him to join us, he does so hate to dine on his own.'

The man frowned and began to feel unsure of himself. 'I, er . . .'

'It'll be perfectly all right,' she interrupted quickly, 'he's my father. Shall we go and choose Mister Dempsey's tie?'

Dempsey leant across the starched double-damask tablecloth and narrowed his eyes. 'You didn't tell me your old man was a dook.'

'He's not a duke, he's a lord, and anyway we haven't really had much time to compare family trees.'

They talked easily together and were on their second drink when Lord Winfield came into the restaurant, with Blake in tow.

'Good God,' Makepeace whispered, 'he's got Mr Blake with him.'

'Who's he?'

'He's Daddy's manservant.'

Lord Winfield came to the table and Dempsey stood up and was introduced.

'I shan't gatecrash, Harriet, my dear. Mr Blake and I have things to discuss, private matters. And so I'll say cheerio. Very nice to have met you, Dempsey, no doubt we'll meet again.'

'Yes sir.'

'Take good care of her – she'll probably make a good policeman one day. Come on, Blake, we're over here, I think,' and the two old men shuffled off to their table.

'He seems quite a guy,' Dempsey said as he sat down, 'but what the hell's he taking his manservant out for?'

'I don't know, it's most odd, unless they've taken my advice.'

'And what was that?'

'Oh – I said that as they were both getting a bit shaky on their pins, especially poor old Mr Blake, they should really work as a team and try and forget the fact that one is more senior than the other.' She looked at Dempsey, 'Rank-wise, that is.'

He looked at her and smiled warmly for the first time. 'Can I call you Harry, Sergeant?'

'Yes please. If I can drop the lootenant bit.'

'My christian name's James, but most of the guys call me Jimmy.'

'You're not really a James or a Jimmy; I think I'll just call you Dempsey – if that's all right.'

He nodded. 'That's fine – now, let's see what this place has got to eat,' and he beckoned the waiter and ordered for them both.

'You wanna brandy with your coffee?'

Makepeace shook her head. 'No – I think I'll have a port, as long as they don't throw it all over me.'

'Listen, if it hadn't been for the port, we wouldn't be here now.'

'If it hadn't been for the port you may very well have been cajoled into the black widow's bed – now there's a sobering thought.'

Dempsey looked at her for a long time and then said, 'Shall I book that room?'

Makepeace looked quizzically at him, and felt somehow schoolgirlish and shy; with her father in the same room and her new American partner making a very attractive proposition.

'That, I think, would be too much for a girl in one day, and besides, rooms here cost an arm and a leg.'

He shrugged. 'Okay, whenever you wanna take me up on it, the offer's there.'

She nodded, and they lapsed briefly into silence, and then she said, 'So you don't speak Italian.'

154

He shook his head. 'No – my mother's great regret was never making me learn. I know enough to get by in an Italian restaurant, but that's all.'

'You should try and learn, it's a beautiful language. The Italians seem able to express themselves in such a delicate way that leaves even the French a poor second.'

They talked on into the evening, and were still in deep conversation long after Lord Winfield had left with Blake.

'Well, Harry old bean,' Dempsey mocked, 'if I can't talk you into staying on, I guess we'd better make tracks. I'll get the bill and we'll go, okay?'

She held his hands across the table and was surprised at how delicate they felt. 'It's just a question of time, Dempsey – but now is too soon.'

'Maybe you're right,' he said, and held on to her hands for a few seconds and their eyes smiled.

The man wore gloves and carried a suitcase. He walked up the flight of stairs that led to the front door of the flat, stopped and listened. Three minutes before, he'd rung the flat from the public box at the end of the road and got no reply. He inspected the door and the lock. It was a single Yale and within twenty seconds he was inside and had closed the door behind him. He went through the flat from room to room and having searched the flat thoroughly, he came back to the front door. He opened it again, inspected the panels on the door and closed it again, softly.

The first class passengers had finished the evening meal, and the cabin staff were dispensing coffee and brandy. Schwartz had started with a champagne cocktail with the salmon, and with the partridge he'd ploughed his way through two bottles of Napa Cabernet Sauvignon and finished off with brandy after the baked Alaska.

'Another brandy, Mr Schwartz?'

He looked up at the one with the alligator smile and

shook his head. 'I don't think so baby.' His voice was just a little slurred, and he grinned back at her. 'I think I'll weave my way to the john and then get some sleep. Gotta be bright-eyed and bushy-tailed for my lawyer tomorrow morning,' and he got to his feet and she escorted him to the toilet.

Half an hour later he'd fallen asleep watching the in-flight movie and was still fast asleep when the film stopped and all the main cabin lights were dimmed. The huge bulbous 747 powered its way towards the cold East Coast of America and inside its pressurized cabin the majority of its passengers, having been fed and watered, slept or dozed in their cramped serried ranks, while the cabin staff cat-napped before the onslaught of breakfast. The aircraft seemed to hang in the sky as if in nocturnal limbo. Schwartz slept deeply, cocooned in alcohol, and in the certain knowledge that his lawyer would prize him like a blackhead from the arms of the law within minutes of clearing immigration.

No-one saw the small slight figure come through from the economy section. No-one saw the figure stop and look down at Schwartz, and Schwartz barely opened his eyes as the needle sank into his arm, administering a massive injection of heroin. He looked up and saw the almond eyes, remote and somehow distant in the twilight of the first class cabin, and his mind and the drink played their tricks of memory and places and faces, and he was in a village somewhere in Laos when he went into terminal coma, and when the early morning smile shook his shoulder, he was already dead.

'I suppose that slightly over a £100 is a lot to pay for dinner, but then you did go over the top a bit with the vino el-plonko.'

'They didn't have any goddamn prices on anything, how was I to know?' said Dempsey crossly.

'The vintage, my dear – gives you a clue.' She

stopped the car outside Marlborough Mansions and looked at her passenger. 'Anyway, it's never really the same paying for something with a credit card, it's like Monopoly money really.'

Dempsey winced. 'You try telling that to my bank manager. Believe me, Harry, they don't just make you miss three turns, and I ain't got no hotels on Park Avenue.'

'Park Lane.'

He grinned and turned to her. 'You wanna coffee?'

She hesitated.

'No strings – just coffee,' and then he added, 'if you're as tired as I am there'd be no point.'

'Okay – one cup and then I must go home.'

They got out of the car and walked up the stairs to the door of his flat. Dempsey fumbled for his key, eventually remembering that it was just a single key and he'd put it in his bill-fold. He put the key in the door and just as he was about to turn it in the lock, he saw the small piece of tissue paper on the floor. The paper he'd jammed between the door and the frame when he'd left on Saturday morning. Slowly he slipped the Magnum from its holster, looked at the small wedge of paper again, then at Makepeace, putting his finger to his lips.

For a second she didn't understand, and then she took out her ·38, thumbed back the hammer and released the safety catch. Dempsey indicated that she should not stand in front of the door and they both stepped back and stood on either side of it.

Slowly Dempsey turned the key in the lock and then said in a loud voice, 'Okay, Harry, let's go and take a look at my etchings,' and he pushed the door open and stood back. As the door swung back on its hinges the silence in the Victorian mansion block was shattered by a long burst of machine-gun fire, and the old plaster from the opposite wall flew around the stairwell in all directions. The blast of fire stopped and Dempsey heard hurried footsteps on the carpet inside the flat.

157

He looked into the hallway of the apartment and saw a figure running down the hall. He fired low and the figure screamed and then stumbled, dropping the weapon as he fell.

Dempsey ran down the hall and kicked the sub-machine gun away and out of the reach of the man on the floor. He'd been hit in the back of the thigh and there was a lot of blood coming from the flesh wound. He rolled over onto his back, sucking in air as though it would make the pain ease, and it was then that Dempsey saw his face. The face behind the windscreen of the Cadillac.

The man looked up and as Dempsey levelled the Magnum at his heart, he spat at Dempsey and said, 'Io sono il primo figlio bastardo del tuo padre morto – queste pietre sono per le tua tasca!'

And he opened his clenched fist and let the stones fall onto the carpet.

Dempsey fired, just once, and the man bucked like a pig in a slaughterhouse and lay dead. Makepeace turned away as the implication of the translation sank in.

'I am the first bastard son of your dead father – these stones are for your pocket.'

Dempsey lowered his gun slowly and looked at Makepeace. 'What'd he say, Harry?'

She shook her head and looked away. 'I couldn't hear – I don't know,' and she wished they'd taken the room.

All Futura Books are available at your bookshop or newsagent, or can be ordered from the following address: Futura Books, Cash Sales Department, P.O. Box 11, Falmouth, Cornwall.

Please send cheque or postal order (no currency), and allow 55p for postage and packing for the first book plus 22p for the second book and 14p for each additional book ordered up to a maximum charge of £1.75 in U.K.

Customers in Eire and B.F.P.O. please allow 55p for the first book, 22p for the second book plus 14p per copy for the next 7 books, thereafter 8p per book.

Overseas customers please allow £1 for postage and packing for the first book and 25p per copy for each additional book.